RELUCTANT CANDIDATE

Vol. 3 The Reluctant President

JACK R. STANLEY

Wrightbridge Press

Copyright © 2019 Jack R. Stanley
All rights reserved.
ISBN: 978-1-947726-55-0

FREE E-BOOKS

[MURDER IN MULESHOE]
There's a murderer in town. Should we track him or her down or throw a parade?

[GUNS ALONG THE RIO]
It's 1852 and two fresh off the ranch 17-year-olds join the Texas Rangers. What could possibly go wrong?

Go To http://eepurl.com/dKEi_Y

DEDICATION

To Mary Lee who makes all things possible.

CHAPTER 1

P otential candidates do not speak at either political party's nominating convention. It's taboo. Verboten. Not kosher. Simply not done.

However, a sitting and outgoing President was expected to give an inspiring, enthusiastic boosting speech on the opening night of his party's convention.

When President Porter Randall stepped up to the podium at the Republican Convention at the Bridgestone Arena in Nashville, Tennessee, he knew that his remarks were not the top news story of the day. He thought of his convention speech to the Republican delegates as a farewell address to the party. And it was. After all, he wasn't a Republican himself.

RANDALL HAD SERVED ALMOST TWO YEARS AS US PRESIDENT BY THE time the next election cycle came around. By tradition the party out-of-power held their presidential nomination convention first in the summer of election years followed by the party in-power. The definition of "in power" was defined by which party controlled the White House.

The custom faced novel circumstances this year. Even as the current media devised their strategies for covering the upcoming election, they were dealing with a never-before scenario. The elected Democrat, Leo B. Gibson, who should have been in the White House, had died in office and was replaced through unique circumstances by an Independent. A political scandal called *"Netgate"* involved politicians of both parties, many of whom were pushing legislation to benefit software makers and computer chip manufacturers. Stock in these companies were held by too many Senators and House Representatives, even appointed officials, all of whom had significant financial stakes in the legislation and its impact.

The infamy of the corruption also entangled the then Republican Speaker-of-the-House, Budd Elliot, who had to resign under fire days before the Christmas break. Before the House could gavel an end to its current session, the majority party had to caucus and pick a replacement. It was the task of the Speaker to officially end the session. Picking a new Speaker was easier said than accomplished.

The next in line to be Speaker was House Majority Leader, Vincent Sturges from Ohio. But his heavy handed style had built resistance against him enough that he was challenged for the job by Majority Whip, Tray Rifkin, from Arizona. The caucus dragged on for hours and vote after vote without either man gaining sufficient support to win.

Sophomore Representative Porter Randall from the Texas Panhandle had been ultimately and surprisingly selected. This came after the legislator had simply offered what he thought was an innocent suggestion to the problem. In short, they should find someone they could agree on to take on the title and the job while the two combatants worked out their differences over the holidays. When Congress reconvened, the agreed upon acting Speaker would then step aside, and one of the two men who now wanted the position, would be officially elected by the new legislature.

Sturges and Rifkin agreed that the Texas Rep would be the ideal person for the job. Although officially an Independent, Randall caucused with the Republicans. When he was called on his suggestion, he very reluctantly accepted the title and position and brought the session to a close. He then returned to the Lone Star State without even visiting the vacant Speaker's office.

Being a very traditional politician, then President Leo Gibson, had been wheeling and dealing as he trolled the waters for a new Vice President over the Christmas break. However, Gibson had died of a brain aneurism while vacationing with influential Hollywood Democrats. By the laws of succession, when there was no Vice President, the Speaker of the House became President. Randall had been awakened in the early hours of the morning by a detail of Secret Service Agents and an Air Force officer carrying the "football" nuclear codes. Reluctantly the Texan accepted his lot, being, in fact, the official Speaker of the House and took on the task of unelected President.

Randall had appointed New Hampshire Governor Sundee Ives, a Democrat, as Vice President. He also retained most of his predecessor's cabinet. So, the nod was given to the Republicans to go first as the party out of power. Most viewed the White House in the hands of the Democrats and therefore "in power."

※

Attempts at a compromise between now House Speaker Vincent Sturges and House Whip, Tray Rifkin to head the Republican ticket — even variations with both on the ticket —would not work. Neither would give ground on their intractable positions.

Rifkin was a wine growing rancher. His characteristic white Stetson and a voice for causes were often considered too moderate for some true GOP mainliners. Speaker Sturges had made enemies and bruised many party members with his bombastic style. Still, he was a leader — to some.

It was already a foregone conclusion that wheelchair bound George Tossen, Senator from California, would be selected next week by the Democrats as their nominee. The seventy year-old with stark white hair and matching snowy mustache, was a distinguished figure even while in his wheel chair. He was respected and beloved by his party thus making the Republicans struggle to find just the right leader for their standard bearer easy.

Over 93 ballots had been taken and still there was no consensus Republican candidate. The last vote had been to draft Porter Randall for the ticket. That was when Republican National Committee Chair, Clement Nance, had video phoned the President back home at his Palo Duro Canyon ranch. The President had jointed his Chief-of-Staff, Grant Newcome, in front of the big screen monitor in the Secret Service shack.

The question was, "Mr. President, would you consider a draft to be the Republican standard bearer for this year's election?" President Randall was not expecting this.

"I'll have to think about it. Mrs. Randall and I will talk it over — tonight. Call us back tomorrow."

CHAPTER 2

The next day, from the "Texas White House," President Porter Randall and First Lady, Deidra, spoke by encrypted video link to Nashville. They sat in chairs of the Secret Service who maintained their on-site office in what was once a ranch vehicle storage shack — refitted with the best communications and surveillance equipment — including the 55 inch screen the First Couple were facing.

Now, 52 and ending his second year as the nation's Chief Executive, Porter, looked through his hazel eyes and gold-rimmed aviator bifocals at the large screen, his dark brown hair streaked with grey. The politically independent former surgeon, turned successful medical novelist, and then two-term US Representative from the Texas Panhandle, sat with his second wife ready for the video call.

Both the President and First Lady were dressed in ranch casual — jeans, cowboy boots, and plaid shirts. The beautiful 51 year-old First Lady had chestnut hair, cut in a bob, a heart shaped face and a lovely body even for a woman half her age. The former wife of Porter's once surgical business partner who had taken his own life years before, Deidra was most well remarked on for her kind and true spirit in spite of her natural beauty.

On the Tennessee end of the call was Clement Nance, Republican Party Chair, with the thick reddish brown hair and prominent Betty Davis eyes. Also in attendance were other members of the party's executive committee's co-chairs — Senator Llyn DeLast from Utah, tall and willowy under a dome of brilliant white hair and her co-vice chair, Senator Hartman Vanderpool of Georgia. Vanderpool sported flaring red and gray eyebrows on his long face. Also in attendance were the two current top candidates.

Although Nance was the head of the party, the stern, often caustic and combative DeLast had made a name for herself championing her parties' positions by taking no prisoners and giving no ground. Porter knew she was there to be heard.

Vanderpool, a former prosecutor and legal scholar was known for his clever and quick wit he used to cut to the heart of matters and carved up opponents. He was popular on cable TV for his insights. Neither of the party co-vice chairs had been able to mount sufficient support for a presidential run themselves. They were making themselves felt through their behind the scenes steering of the brand.

Seated at the far end of the table, farthest from the video camera, were the two candidates, House Speaker Vincent Sturges and House Whip, Tray Rifkin. The younger, wiry, 45 year-old Rifkin was more moderate than the hard rock, quick tempered and often controversial Sturges. But they were still the top contenders and were not going to give in easily.

Nance had used his pleasant but almost raspy voice to act as spokesman for the group.

"Mr. President, Mrs. Randall — you've had overnight to think it over. What is your answer? Will you accept a draft and be the top of our ticket?"

It was a good, clean connection between the Nashville hotel room and the President's ranch. That was important because Porter and Deidra wanted to make sure everyone understood each other.

"I will," Porter began but quickly added, "— under certain conditions."

"So, this is a negotiation?" Senator DeLast asked already on the defensive.

"Were you expecting a 'Yes' or 'No' answer?" Porter responded.

"It's a simple question, Mr. President. We're asking you to be our standard bearer — which means you would be running as a candidate for our ticket."

"I've given you my 'Yes,' but there are some conditions. Isn't that what this smoke-filled room is all about?"

"Nobody's smoking, and it depends on your conditions," the Georgia Senator, Vanderpool, said curtly, his eyebrows almost leaping off his long face.

"Of course, you understand that our party platform has already been crafted and accepted by the delegates," DeLast cut in not wanting to yield any power. "There's not a lot we can do about that."

"Then," the President said, "the answer is 'No.' Period — full stop."

Trying to take back control and aware of the struggle the party and the convention had faced this past week, Clement Nance leaned in and spoke calmly. "We can always made accommodations," he said looking around the table.

"Let's hear what those *accommodations* are," Vanderpool said folding his arms.

"First of all," Porter said, "I pick my own running mate."

"See?" Vincent Sturges said gesturing toward the camera. "I told you he was not a team player."

"What if my choice happened to be you, Vincent? Would you still object?"

"I would," Tray Rifkin vehemently replied as his mouth tightened.

"And what if it were you I picked, Tray?" the President asked.

"Then I'd have no objection. Would it be me?"

"I won't tell you until we have a complete understanding — from everyone."

There was silence on both ends of the video conference before Nance tried to exert control again.

"Let's get it all out on the table. What other conditions do you propose?"

"I'm not proposing negotiating positions, these are my deal breakers," Porter said glancing over at his wife who nodded her head.

"You feel like you're in a position to set 'deal breakers'?" DeLast said narrowing her eyes and bracing for a fight.

"Let's understand each other at the very beginning," Porter said. "I had no plans to run for this office — in fact I never sought it."

"But you sure as hell took it when it was offered!" Speaker Sturges all but shouted.

"The position was never '*offered*,'" Porter shot back. "It was presented to me as a done deal. By law, according to what the Secret Service told me, I *was* the President the moment Leo Gibson died."

"But you weren't the real Speaker of the House."

"At that moment, who held the position?" Porter asked calmly.

Sturges sulked back in his chair. This was an old argument which had been brewing from the first moment Sturges was informed. He went on to win the position of Speaker before the new Congress had convened, but he knew full well that by the letter and the spirit of the law, Porter Randall was both Speaker and therefore President.

Turning back to the rest of the table, Porter said, "I have never had presidential ambitions. You are not doing me any favors by asking me to accept your party's nomination. I am, and always have been, an Independent. But if I were to take on your party's label, you will have to make it worth my while."

"Can we, please," Llyn DeLast said imperially, "cut to the fucking chase? What are your other deal breakers?"

"Only one. We all know the proposed Constitutional Amendments will never get out of Congress — even out of committee."

"So?" Nance said cocking his head as if trying to get a better view of the situation.

"If I run, the two amendments, numbers 28 and 29, the Congressional Term Limits and the Balanced Budget Amendment will also be on the ballot. They don't have to be part of the party platform, but I want them *on* the ballot in every state. Then the people will decide it these amendments pass or fail."

Before anyone else could respond, Clement Nance said, "These are serious considerations. I think they are best discussed face to face. Mr. President, can you come to Nashville?"

"Clement," Porter said, "it cost $228,000 dollars an hour to fly Air Force One. If I come to Nashville, that's 2 hours both ways. Do the math. And if I fly in, there's no keeping it a secret. Then there's the problem of getting a "helicopter lift package" back to Nashville. They're already back in DC — and there's another here in Texas. I can't just move around at ease. You all know this. I am required to use Air Force One, Marine One and The Beast. That's never going to be stealthy."

"It doesn't matter," Llyn DeLast said firmly. "We're never going to agree to your deal breakers. Too much of our party's efforts are devoted to keeping party members in elected positions — your amendments would severely hamper our efforts in that sphere. Seniority in Congress would be shot to hell."

"I'm thinking it should be," Porter said.

"Really? Term Limits *and* Balanced Budget? You're living in fantasy land, Mr. President."

Both sides of the conference call were silent for a long moment. Finally, Porter said, "I think that wraps up our business."

"You're damn right it does," Senator Sturges blurted out.

"Then let's not waste any more of anybody's time," the President suggested.

After glancing around the table, Clement Nance turned back to the camera and said, "Thank you for considering it, Mr. President."

"I honestly wish you the best of all possible outcomes with your efforts," Porter said. "Good-bye."

The screen on both ends went black.

IN NEW YORK CITY IN A CONFERENCE ROOM ON THE TOP FLOOR OF the INK Building, all the powers of that cable news organization were together. The session was packed with standing room only — anchors and senior producers had the only chairs in the channel's largest conference room. Perfume and colognes mixed and there were a couple of sneezes in the cloistered gathering.

"The story is — the Republicans are in disarray. They're confused, ideologically in shambles. Their whole convention is a dumb and dumber's joke"

Shaggy-headed forty-year-old owner and Senior Executive Editor, Zeb Tolle, addressed his troops — on-the-air anchors, producers, news writers and other staff.

Intercontinental News Key (INK) was Tolle's most-recent acquisition, 10 years ago, and his favorite toy. The once wunderkind of social media software, holding a dozen and a half patents of the world's more popular apps, now thought of himself as a latter-day Citizen Kane. He was going to remold the world in his image of truth as he saw it through the power of news. INK's slogan was "The Most Responsible Name In News."

"They can neither get their shit together nor nominate a single leader to run against the Democrat's George Tossen," Tolle continued.

"Can we quote you on that?"

The question came from Howard X. Sterling, INK's dean of all anchors. The three-time Pulitzer Prize winning broadcast journalist was, as always, on-the-air picture perfect in a starched buttoned-down light blue shirt with dark tie and vest. As renowned as Sterling was, the man was also known to be not only approachable but always ready with a quip to keep conversations light or at least in perspective.

The boss, Zeb Tolle, didn't appreciate humor, especially at his expense. His preference was for dark humor that exposed and possibly humiliated others. His jaw tightened as a few snickers were heard throughout the room.

"They are out of sync with the American public," Tolle went on ignoring the interruption, "and it's reflected in their indecision. Now, go collect your facts and report this as your storyline."

Again, Howard Sterling spoke up.

"The profession I learned was that we report the facts — clear and unbiased — and let the public decide what it means."

"That's the old journalism, Howard. This is the new world journalism. Wake up and smell the bacon."

The room was silent as the 60 year-old anchor turned his head slightly and closed his eyes a moment. When he opened them, he said,

"What about your memo about our not using the term 'bacon' because it offended some people?"

Producers, writers and other reporters were biting their lips to keep from laughing.

"Howard, if you want to set policy, buy your own network," Tolle said narrowing his eyes at the most highly paid person on the network.

"Well, maybe it's just me," Sterling said. "It could be that I'm too damn old to learn the *new* journalism."

"Do you like your $52 million a year? Do you like working here?"

The room was silent as everyone held their breath. They knew Howard was well paid but not that well paid.

"The money's okay," Howard said. "And I used to love it here. A great deal. But not so much these days."

Now it was Zeb Tolle who had everyone's attention.

"Howard, you know where the front door is. You don't have to let it hit you in the ass as you leave!" Tolle's voice got louder and shriller with every word. "And you have my permission to pack your things and leave at any time!"

The radioactive tension level in the room was suddenly at critical. Everyone's boss had threatened their most respected member.

Howard looked down at the conference table, put his hands on it, and stood.

"I guess that time would be — now," he said and walked out.

Saundra Fontan, Howard's longtime producer and head writer, looked from the closing door to Tolle who stood at the head of the table with his mouth slightly open. The middle-aged blonde-haired woman got to her feet saying, "Uh — Howard didn't mean that. You didn't mean that, Zeb. I'll go talk to him."

"I meant every single word I said!" Tolle shot at the producer as the walnut door closed.

Some of those in the crowded room had their hands over their mouths and their eyes wide open. Had they just seen what they thought they had?

CHAPTER 3

The firing of Howard X. Sterling from Intercontinental News Key was breaking news all over the world. By the afternoon, it was the whole A-block of every cable, internet, and broadcast news channel in the Western World. In the few remaining newspapers, the story was front page, above the fold — the lead story.

Sterling was mostly remembered as the steady, stoic, restrained emotional, on-the-scene reporter when terrorists crashed passenger jets into the World Trade Center. He was soon after made a news anchor and had become what only Walter Cronkite had achieved by the middle of the last century. He was the one voice of reason and truth in an age were journalists everywhere seemed to have lost their ethics and their compass.

Sterling had disappeared after his exit from INK and made no statements — issued no press releases. His producer Saundra Fontana was seen coming and going to INK New York studios, but she would not take any questions. The mystery of why Sterling had left only grew as Republicans continued their convention.

"Zeb, you fired him in front of a room of 36 people."

"All of whom depend on me for a pay check."

"You don't want to go there." David Garcia, early 60's, over weight, bulbous nose and a thin attempt at a Van Dyke beard that never filled in, was INK's lead legal counsel. "No matter how well you think you've pulled it off, someone's going to leak it. Then you've lost big time."

"Then you tell me what we do? I'm not paying that son-of-a-bitch $52 million dollars a year to do nothing!"

"You should have thought of that before you cut him loose."

"There is another way to look at it," Garcia's partner in law and what was often just barely legal crime, Alfie Brown, said. Brown was as thin as Garcia was fat. The Mutt and Jeff pair were known to be a no-holds-barred team who sometimes gave the terms, *ambulance-chaser*, *shyster*, and *shark* a bad name. They were multi-millionaires because of their minor stake in Tolle's empire. Garcia and Brown were Zeb's legal A-team. They'd successfully suffocated and crushed start-ups with false copyright and bogus patent infringement claims against younger companies who could have potentially been competitors. Usually, under the avalanche of legal claims, the companies couldn't afford to litigate. Most were forced to declare bankruptcy.

"Think of it as paying to keep him off the air," Brown continued. "As long as you do, he can't go to work for anyone else."

"But $52 million."

"Zeb, that's chump change to you," Garcia said.

"Well, yeah," Tolle admitted, "but still --."

"Let it go. You've got too many other things on your mind to waste the energy and time on Sterling."

"That's true." Then after a moment more thought, Zeb said, "All right. The hell with him. But if you guys can think of anything to sue him for, I want to know about it."

"No, you don't," Alfie said. "If you go after him, it will be seen as Goliath chasing a flea. Zeb, you've won. He's out. He can't work for anyone else. And it's no longer a pain in your ass."

Finally the shaggy headed grump let out a long sigh and slumped back in his chair.

"Screw him."

SAUNDRA FONTAN, HOWARD STERLING'S LONG TIME TV PRODUCER was seated in her former boss's midtown penthouse living room. She was middle-aged, blonde with hints of grey at her roots. She was a pleasant looking woman but serious and intelligent. She wore a dark skirt, a taupe blouse, and a small gold cross on a chain around her neck. She held a cup of coffee which the wife of her host, Jessica Jackson Sterling, had just poured.

Jessica radiated internal beauty which was captivating and endearing to everyone she met. Her hair was steel grey but worn in a soft cut just above her shoulders. She filled Howard's cup and sat beside him on the other couch facing the one their guest occupied.

"Do you miss the work or the pay check?" Howard asked. He wore a light blue button down oxford dress shirt and tie. His blue suspenders gave him the appearance of a journalist in the middle of the day.

"Both," she said. "But we both know I am on no one's poverty list. I could do without the pay check, but as a single woman there are still things I'd like to do and places I'd like to see. Money always helps in those endeavors." She took a sip of coffee. "But I've been working all my adult life — I picked career over marriage and family — so you'd have to say I *do* miss the work."

"What do they have you doing at work?"

"They're trying to get me to mentor some of the other producers. Zeb has given me the title of Senior Executive Producer. That means I was given a slightly bigger office, a new name plate on my door, and a great deal of free time — other producers don't like an interfering old lady in their business.

"By the by, have you seen your replacement?" she asked.

"I haven't looked at INK since I passed the last monitor at the front door on my way out."

"Not that you've missed much — but you should see what Zeb is putting in your place — California pretty boy, very symmetrical face, more hair than God ever intended, glasses he doesn't need, double last name — Yancy Day-French. Wonderful voice — which no one enjoys more than he does — very progressive and very free with his opinions — goes off script whenever he feels the urge. The sponsors love him — but the public is still making up its mind. First ratings were a disaster, but they've climbed out of the toilet a little."

"Okay," Howard said with deep concern, "but what do you really think?"

Saundra and Jessica burst out laughing while Howard maintained his seemingly serious expression — until he finally dropped it and let a small smile paint his face from his lips to his eyes.

"Well, given all that, how'd you like to come to work for me? Double your salary and co-author credit on several books?"

"Whoa. Double? The money sounds good — but I've never written a book."

"Neither have I," Howard said with a slight smile. "That doesn't mean we can't do it. We've had too many years and too much experience not to write some of it down."

"Where would we work?"

"Here — and at your house, if it's okay with you. We could even get an office somewhere if you like. We both know we can write on a laptop or tablet anywhere. God knows we've done it long enough."

"And what would we write, Howard?"

"First of all I'd like to expose the state of journalism — and then we could tackle anything we decided we want."

Saundra took another sip of coffee.

"Aside from being the best offer I've had today — or this week, I kind of like it. I certainly don't fit in Zeb Tolle's world anymore." She turned to Howard's wife. "Jessica, how are you with this?"

"It was my idea," she said with a twinkle. "I've been sharing my husband with you for over 30 years. What you do for him, what you two do together, is something I can't compete with and don't even want to try. If Howard's not working, he's going to be underfoot. Like Irma Bombeck said to her husband after he retired, 'I married you for better or worse — but not for lunch. *Get out of my house!*'"

They all shared a laugh.

Teasingly Saundra said, "You'll just have to promise me, Jessica, you won't try to fix me up with somebody."

"I'll promise not to force anything on you, Saundra, but there are some people I know I'd like for you to know. What, if anything, ever comes of it is none of my business."

"Okay, okay," Saundra smiled. "But understand I'm not looking for another man — your husband is enough for me — as long as you don't mind sharing his brains and humor – you can keep the rest."

"Suddenly," Howard said, "I feel very tawdry and cheap."

"Not to worry, dear" Jessica grinned. "You'll always be high maintenance."

"Oh, *that* does make me feel *so much* better."

They shared a good laugh once more.

."

"Have I ever?" Jessica toasted Saundra with her cup.

"Then I guess we're *Hasenpfeffer Incorporated*."

"The name may already be copyrighted, but we'll find something," Howard said. "I do have a book title — Requiem For Journalism."

"I like it!"

CHAPTER 4

It was Trey Rifkin who finally gave in and accepted the Republican number two spot on the ticket. This solidified the party's slate and put icy white haired and bushy eye browed, 70 year-old, Vincent Sturges, Representative from Ohio, and House Majority Leader as the Republican choice for President.

Clement Nance, Republican Party Chair, along with Senator Llyn DeLast from Utah, and her co-vice chair, Senator Hartman Vanderpool of Georgia had used all their considerable persuasive powers, logic, and pleading to convince Rifkin to step aside. The 44 year-old California avocado rancher in his characteristic white Stetson, had accepted the logic that this was not his year. However, after 8 years as Vice President, Rifkin would be in a position to do what few running mates had ever done, namely following their predecessor into the White House. The years as VP would give Rifkin time to polish his image and position himself as a behind the scenes leader who could get things done.

What few knew as that for all his speeches and proclamations, Trey Rifkin was a lazy man. He didn't like having to work for things he could acquire with a minimum of effort. The VP job seemed to him to be just such a position. He was enough of a politician to be able and willing to parrot Vincent Sturges's slogans and talking points as long as it produced the winning combination they both were after. As VP, Rifkin knew he would have few actual responsibilities and many perks. An 8 year vacation was how he viewed the job — but he was finally willing to accept it.

The convention ended, the confetti and the balloons fell, and the wheels began to turn out all the materials, signs, hats, buttons, and t-shirts of the campaign. The serious business of devising solutions for fund raising and developing the strategies a presidential run would require had long been underway behind the scenes. For two weeks the Republicans mostly held their fire while the Democrats convened and selected their ticket.

AS FOR THE DEMOCRATS, OUT OF A CROWDED FIELD OF WANT-A-BES, wheelchair bound Senator George Tossen from California, had quickly emerged as the clear nomination winner. The rarely bombastic but logical and clear spoken *Lionheart of the Senate*, as he was called by the progressive media, was portrayed as a modern day FDR. His slogan was "A Lion and a Heart for America." Posters reminiscent of the FDR 1932 campaign were almost a copy of an old newspaper picture with a cameo of Tossen looking like that of Roosevelt — never showing the wheelchair.

The surprise was Amelia Morris, the "new, *bright shiny, thing*" — a first term House Representative from Massachusetts. The just barely 35 and eligible Morris was attractive and garnered more than her share of media attention because of her sometimes outlandish and Socialist leaning ideas and pronouncements. She was the darling of younger voters who knew little about the horrific history of socialism's swath of tragedy across the world. To those who thought in simple phrases and simpler ideas, she was the right voice at the right time.

It didn't hurt that Amelia Morris was short, just five foot one, and was almost head to head with Tossen standing beside the Presidential candidate. It was easy to photograph the two without including Tossen's wheelchair.

Universally proclaimed to be a *"bleeding heart liberal,"* she was easily the "heart" of the slogan.

Party leaders and Tossen himself got an "in writing" agreement to "stick to the script" which would be prepared for her by campaign and party officials. The biggest fear was that Morris would go off unprepared and make gaphs which could tie up the campaign and the media messaging for weeks with an off-the-cuff comment. Amelia Morris was smart enough to understand what was being asked of her, but she also understood the power that would await her after winning an election as Vice President.

Gordon Lewellyn, the mustached, thin lipped, former Black Panther agitator, now chair of the Democratic National Committee, was eager for the fight. Although he would much rather have someone black on the ticket, he knew he could work his will with both Tossen and Morris. Lewellyn played dirty, always had, and he had some tricks he was ready to deploy in the fight ahead.

And so the lines were drawn and the campaigns began.

The slogan for the Democrats was *A Better Future*. The Republicans went with *A New Beginning*.

Media ads rolled out and posters were revealed touting the names and the faces of the candidates. The Republicans started their ground game in New York while the Democrats began in California. The next week they each shifted to opposite coasts. Eventually the Democrats focused on the Rust Belt and the Old South as the Republicans hopscotched across the Midwest and the west.

The Democratic message was, in effect, "We can give you more of everything." The Republicans went for "Lower taxes and less regulation." The media, with few exceptions, played it as "Same ol', same ol'" for the Republicans and "Forward thinking/innovative ideas" for the Democrats.

Pundits for both sides screamed and ranted their messages on cable and the Internet. Social media stars and talk radio drew deep lines of demarcation and mounted and plugged the talking points for their choice.

The public seemed little engaged because, as one poll revealed, many believed this was rerun politics from the elite with little impact on the general public. The Democrats superior ground game brought out the crowds for rallies and said little when there were physical clashes between their followers and those on the Republican side.

Try as they would, the mouth pieces and media platforms had little success in stirring up public opinion one way or the other. It was as if the electorate was tired of the division, the mudslinging, and the overall negativity of the election season. The heat of early summer was oppressive and it manifested itself in the lackluster attitude of the public. It was only the far fringes of each party who seemed to much care about the whole process.

Howard Sterling and Saundra Fontan, his former on-the-air producer, knocked out their first chapter which set the tone of the book and outlined the material to follow. They were satisfied with it and divided up their needed research for the rest of the book. Unknown to Howard, Saundra began shopping their book with publishers based on the first chapter. Within a week there was a bidding war in full force.

"Are we ready for this?" she asked her co-author before Saundra began making return calls to publishers.

"You're the producer," Howard had said. "Produce."

Three days later they were flooded with offers.

"Do you know what sold it?" she asked. Not waiting for an answer she went on, "It was the comment about what JFK wanted in a mistress."

"'Brainy, but not too smart, like a journalist.'" Howard quoted.

"And you see what kind of buzz we're getting," Saundra smiled. "They can't wait until we have more. We need to strike while you're hot, Howard."

"Hot? I've never been called that?"

"Jessica has!"

"Well, she's my wife. She has to."

"Oh *contrair*," Jessica said from the doorway, carrying a carafe of fresh coffee and warm scones on a tray. "I don't recall such a clause in my vows."

"See," Saundra said standing and taking the tray.

"Sorry, but being *hot* was never a professional goal," Howard grinned.

"So much the better," Jessica said with a wink.

"You, sweetheart, are the one who is hot," Howard smiled, "— and always have been. That's one of the reasons I was attracted to you."

"And here I thought it was my brain."

"You do have a hot brain, my love — more than me. I'm just a journalist."

"Do I thank you or JFK?" she asked. She leaned down and gave Howard a kiss. "I'm with Saundra."

"I leave that side of it up to her completely," Howard said. "All I'm interested in is getting the book done."

"Here's my chapter three," Saundra said handing Howard a stack of 20 pages and a red flash drive."

"All right," he said, "picking up a stack of his own, "here's chapter 2." He gave her a green flash drive.

"What? Have you two divided it up chapter by chapter?" Jessica asked.

"Some of it. We both have the same vision — and a lot of it is merely a matter of getting it down on paper."

"And you know I write like Howard after all this time," Saundra said.

"But you must have some input on each chapter?"

"Oh, we both do," Howard said picking up a draft of their first chapter. It was covered with red marks and black inserts.

"Whose is what?" Jessica said flipping through the pages.

"I'm red," Saundra said, "Howard's black — but in the end you can't tell which is which."

"So, I see."

"The important thing is that word is now out and regardless of the bidding, there is already an audience for the book. And I'll bet Zeb Tolle is having a fit."

They all burst into laughter at the idea.

※

"I'VE GOT TO SUE OVER THIS!" THE INTERNATIONAL NEWS KEY CEO roared. "He signed a non-compete agreement."

"Problem is, we don't know he's violated his NCA," Alfie Brown, the smaller of his two-attorney team, said. "We certainly can once we see anything he's said about you or the operation here."

"But not before, Zeb," David Garcia chimed in. "For all we know —"

"We don't know shit!" Zeb shouted. "We can't wait until it's published!"

"That's all we *can* do," Brown said. "Until something is out there, he's not violated anything."

"Damn him!" Zeb thundered blistering red in the face.

"Don't let him control the narrative," Garcia suggested. "You have some material on Sterling — some material which can damage him, don't you?"

"I have people working on it," Zeb admitted slowly. "I'm not pleased with what they have come up with, yet. But they're still working."

"Keep them at it. When the time comes, we'll need everything they'll develop."

CHAPTER 5

As the conventions continued, in the White House it was business as usual — which meant nothing was usual. World and the different national crisis events dictated the actions of America's Chief Executive more than any program or well thought out approach to a given problem.

White House Chief-of-Staff, 31 year-old Graham Newcome, had light blue eyes, a rail thin body and quick mind. He had been Porter's Chief-of-Staff back in the House of Representatives. He came with Porter to the White House but quickly realized he was in way over his head. He had taken on the job of Porter's congressional liaison. However, when Victor Chesterfield resigned the post, Graham had accepted the promotion to the White House Chief-of-Staff.

He stepped up to the job and performed admirably. He saw himself as a servant of his nation in a job for the President. He kept the West Wing of the White House humming and looked forward to each new day.

Graham was aware that the Republicans had tried to harness Porter's star to their wagon and that Porter had walked away from it. He had seen a few of the old remaining Gibson staff members resign their White House posts to go support the Democrats in the upcoming campaign.

Chief among them was Grant Yarbrough. The former CNN news anchor had been Press Secretary to Gibson and was in California when the former President died of a sudden brain aneurysm. Grant, the son of a Vietnamese mother and a father who was a black US Air Force sergeant, had inherited the best of both races. His looks and his winning demeanor had served him well, and he had almost fallen under Porter Randall's spell but had extracted himself in time to rejoin the Democratic faithful to support George Tossen.

Learning from Victor Chesterfield, now in his new role as Secretary of Defense, Graham held himself apart from the rest of the White House staff and became a constant observer of all those around him. As such he'd come to be admired by several of them — but Graham neither knew nor cared.

He had come to count on the wisdom and the faithfulness of the now 37-year-old beauty, Cinnamon Higdon, Porter's Director of White House Communications. The five foot seven, coal dark haired woman had striking features with indeterminate heritage — perhaps part African and Korean, or perhaps Arabian and Oriental. She was a stabilizing force of clear vision with intensity and intelligence. First in her class at Stanford Law School, she, like Graham, was a confident of the President.

The Chief-of-Staff caught himself one day thinking, "If I were only a more handsome man..." But he wasn't and he couldn't allow himself to go down that road. He knew he never did well with the ladies — and especially those as classy as Cinnamon. He cleared his mind and got back to business.

United the White House Staff had come together to make the tenure of the "unelected President" one of honor and accomplishment. For the political professionals, Graham observed some looking forward to each new day and occasionally even smiling to themselves. This was a very different world for all of them.

Graham knew something was going on in which he was not involved. The President and First Lady had an off the books meeting with unknown visitors in Trowbridge House. Victor had not been included in the meeting but knew if and when it was time, he would be brought in on what was happening. It surprised him that he didn't feel in the least threatened by these events. Graham had never trusted another person the way he discovered he trusted Porter Randall.

THE PRESIDENT AND FIRST LADY HELD HANDS AS THEY WALKED through the tunnel from the White House under Pennsylvania Avenue to Blair House. They were accompanied by three Secret Service officers, beefy, crew cut, Joe Lamb, and short haired Melissa McBride, both of whom had been there the night Porter learned he had become President. The third was balding, Bryant Polaski, Lamb's new partner. The First Couple emerged in Blair House and followed the usher, small, 53 year-old, and wiry haired Norman Brantley, through connected hallways to Trowbridge House.

The historic house was adjacent to and abutting Blair House around the corner to the South. Trowbridge House sat between Blair House and the Presidential Townhouse, a residence reserved primarily for former Presidents. Trowbridge, a mechanical engineer, military officer, and naturalist, built the house in 1859 and sold it ten years later. It was leased by the US government until it was purchased in 1959.

Mr. Brantley showed the President and First Lady to a comfortable sitting room where three men and a woman awaited them.

Porter, of course, knew Alder Mathers, the ultra-rich Oklahoma oilman. It had been Mathers who had financed and seen to the production of a film Porter had outlined. The story was about the fate of second generation European Muslims who became radicalized by ISIS. Mathers, a full blooded Choctaw, who was said to be richer than God, preferred his anonymity and to work silently behind the scenes of power. The open faced man with large hands and warm eyes had no agenda other than to help Porter succeed.

The big man took Deidra's offered hand, saying, "Mrs. Randall, it's a real pleasure. You have brought true grace to the White House."

"Thank you," she said.

"Mr. President, I want to introduce you to three people whom, I'm sure, you've never heard of. Together we're calling ourselves The Group of Four. First, Mrs. Alice Niesson."

The diminutive lady of about 60 with a full head of short blond hair was dressed in an understated but fashionable pale green suit. She shook hands with first Deidra and then Porter.

"Mrs. Niesson," Porter said.

"And Deacon Vaughn," Alder Mathers said stepping over to a light skinned black man who was about 60.

"Mr. Vaughn," Deidra said and Porter repeated.

"And this is Elliot Mara."

A white haired man with a thin face and alert blue eyes stepped forward.

"Mrs. Randall," he said and then to Porter, "Mr. President."

"Let's sit," Porter said with introductions finished.

Alder Mathers spoke first. "I appreciate your taking this meeting, Mr. President and you, too, Mrs. Randall. As always I have been very secretive about the purpose." Mathers took a breath before he said, "Now that the party conventions are over and the presidential campaign has begun, it has become crystal clear to us —" he gestured to the others in the group, "— that we must act. And *we* are ready to do so." Mathers took a breath and then continued, "If the amendments you've proposed are ever to be passed, you, Mr. President, will have to run for office."

This remark caught both Deidra and Porter completely off guard.

"Before you say anything," Mrs. Alice Niesson cut in, "please hear us out. We understand this is a decision you are going to have to make together, but — we have some considerations we hope you take into account."

Porter and Deidra exchanged a look, nodded and sat back in their upholstered chairs.

"All of us here," Mathers picked up the conversation, "are wealthy — very wealthy. And it's because we've been able to live the American dream — something we see slipping away and which won't be available to future generations — if we don't do something now. That's the only selfish motive in our proposal, I assure you. We are not greedy, power seeking, or ambitious. That's why you've not heard of any of your other guests, Mr. President. They have worked very hard to shield themselves from publicity and notoriety of any kind. You won't even know the good they have done with their wealth because they always act anonymously. We are not here for ourselves — God knows we have more than we ever expected — and probably more than we can ever make use of. However, we all feel very strongly that as St. Luke said, 'For unto whomsoever much is given, of him shall be much required...' and you, Mr. President, the second half of that verse, '... and to whom men have committed much, of him they will ask the more.'"

The room was silent for a moment before the oilman went on.

"We are very aware that you never sought nor wanted the office you hold, Mr. President. But we see God's hand in this — and in your life. We believe that you are the good man our nation needed at this point in history. And we are glad you stepped up to the task with humility and strength. But we think more is being asked of you — both of you."

Deacon Vaughn spoke up next.

"We are not religious fanatics, Mr. President, but people who feel very blessed and therefore feel very responsible. We are coming to you to do what none of us could do but which needs doing."

Finally it was white haired Elliot Mara's turn.

"We have watched carefully what you have done as leader of our nation and the ways in which you have accomplished what you have. It is our belief that more is required of you and we are here to ask you to please take up the challenge."

"Mr. President," Alder Mathers took over the conversation at that point, "you are aware that there was an Exploratory Committee set up in your name several months ago without your permission or involvement. That was our doing. We knew that if, and we understood it was a big '*if*' you decided to run, you would need funds and an organization. Unbeknownst to you, you have a considerable war-chest on which to draw. There will be more funds available if you actually decide to do this.

"We have even begun the process of creating a third political party. An independent party — and that's its name — Independent. Its color is purple — a combination of red and blue — although we are sure some in the media will claim it to be a *royal* purple -- it is not."

Mrs. Niesson spoke up.

"We considered naming it the Bull Moose party after Teddy Roosevelt's third party — but Deacon pointed out that on the ballot it would come out, D for Democrats, R for Republicans and BM for Bull Moose." She smiled.

Deacon Vaughn said, "We thought there would be enough people trying to dump on the idea without our giving them an obvious opening."

"So we thought better of it," Mrs. Niesson concluded.

There was a chuckle from the group.

"We have the resources; we can get you the funds and," Elliot Mara said, "— all we need is for you, Mr. President — and, of course, you, Mrs. Randall, to agree to run."

Porter and Deidra seem to study each other for a moment. Then a ghost of a smile appeared on Deidra's lips.

"We have discussed this," Porter said turning back to the group. "I don't know if you were aware but the Republicans approached us when their convention looked like it couldn't settle on either Sturges or Rifkin."

"Yes, sir," Mathers said, "we were aware. You might say we even had a hand in the offer — but unfortunately the party was not willing to meet your demands. Those events spurred us to be here today."

"And, as I understand it, you are willing to accept my terms?"

"Fact is," Mathers said, "your terms are our terms. We especially want your amendments on the ballot."

"Then let's talk about the nitty gritty of all of this," Porter said. "Party and campaign organization — personnel — legal aspects."

"We have a first class legal team who has been working on all of this since we formed the Exploratory Committee. Within 72 hours we can have you on the ballot in all 50 states plus all the territories. I'm sure you're not up on who's who in the world of political campaigns — but we are. And some of the top names in the field have been off the market to both the Democrats and the Republicans — much to their joint displeasure. These folks have laid out the structure for a third party and are ready to put it all in place."

"All right, how about a vice presidential candidate?" Porter asked.

"We have some ideas along those lines," Mather said producing a folded piece of paper which he handed to Porter, "but we thought you would have your own ideas."

"I do," Porter said accepting the offered list and only glancing at it.

"And jumping ahead a little, do you realize you already have the best campaign advantage of any one? Namely Air Force One."

"I'd rather not use that."

The elder member of the group, Elliot Mara spoke up.

"You don't have much of a choice there, Mr. President. You are still President and as such you have to travel as the President — with all that entails. And at $228,000 dollars an hour, the campaign already has a major outlay of funds to cover that from day one."

"And we can cover it," Mrs. Niesson said. "We've thought this thing through rather thoroughly and are prepared financially and legally for almost every contingency."

Porter and Deidra faced each other and she offered him her hand. Porter sighed and looked back at the group.

"It must be understood from the outset that I will not grant any special favors or special access because of this."

"We expected nothing less," Mathers said. "We don't need anything, Mr. President. It is our position that we are offering what we can for the good of the country — not to line our pocketbooks or gain any advantage. This country has been a blessing to us and we want to return the favor — with no strings attached. We will be totally hands off. After today you will not see or hear from us again — unless you seek us out."

After a few moments of silence in the sitting room, Porter spoke again. "I don't want to use any dirty tricks. I know it's a standard practice, but it's not the way we roll."

"Understood," Mathers said.

Deacon Vaughn said, "You need to understand, Mr. President, that you will still have a Dirty Tricks department — but their function is to respond to the antics of the opposition and to keep you clean and on the straight and narrow."

"Agreed," Porter said. He turned to look at his wife and after getting a small smile and nod from her, the President turned and said, "Okay we're in."

When Porter and Deidra adjourned to lunch back at the White House, Porter said, "You're sure about this?"

"Like it or not," she said, "I think it's your destiny. Neither of us realized it, but, Porter, I think you were born for this."

"I don't know about that," he said.

"You'd better," she smiled. "If we're going to do this, we'd best be on board 100%."

"Agreed."

Porter pulled out the list Mathers had given him and showed it to the First Lady.

"Some interesting choices here," he said.

"Very," Deidra added.

"I'm aware that politics is really not my strong suite. So, perhaps we'll need someone who is very steeped in it."

"And who will be our campaign manager?"

"Mathers said his name is Ward Adair. Ever heard of him?"

"No."

"I have. He and his wife have been complete opposites when it comes to politics. They've worked for competing campaigns in the same race before. He's Midwest, blue collar, fly over country, and she's big city, urban, white collar, and female."

"What's her name?" the First Lady asked.

"Ella Suzuki."

"Oh, yes, I've heard of her. She's been on several daytime talk shows. She's pretty and has a quick wit."

"That's her."

"Are they opposed to each other now?"

"Mathers didn't say. I will find out when I meet Adair."

"When and where."

"Tomorrow. Over in Blair House."

"Am I included?"

"I'd like you to be in on everything."

"Of course," Deidra said with a warm smile.

"And we need to keep all of this to ourselves until after we talk to Adair."

"How are you going to announce your candidacy?"

"I'm hoping our campaign manager has some ideas about that."

<hr>

THAT AFTERNOON IN THE OVAL OFFICE, PORTER SIGNED AN executive order returning the Secret Service from under the Office of Homeland Security to the Treasury Department. He did this without anyone knowing about his and Deidra's campaign decision.

Porter had concluded that the once elevated status of the Secret Service had been diluted as it had become a minor entity under Homeland. By moving it back to the Treasury Department, the service once again became a premier functioning bureau. It was also made independent, although it still reported to Homeland to insure a free flow of information back and forth between the agencies.

The order became a campaign issue for only a moment. Both parties dished the move but couldn't identify specific reasons why the change was bad. The media leaped on the matter and all their pundits slammed the order, but the reasons they were able to articulate were both bizarre and light on substance. After a single day, the subject disappeared from view.

The news cycle was upset with the sudden death of Supreme Court Chief Justice, Brandon Zackery in a fishing camp in Colorado. Zackery had been an Associate Justice when the death of another justice had left an opening. It had been Porter's idea to have the members of the court select one of the current members to take on the role of Chief Justice as opposed to his naming a new, outside person to take on the position. Zackery had the support of his fellow Associate Justices and when nominated by the President, it was one of the quickest confirmations ever seen in DC. But with the new Chief Justice's death the top position was once again open.

Karie Ann Cantu, Porter's pick for the previous vacancy was

already on the court as an Associate Justice. She had been a middle-of-the road choice which neither the Democrats nor the Republicans felt the need to challenge. Now, however, the option for an *"unelected President"* to fill a second seat was a lightning rod.

The immediate reaction from the media and political voices within the DC beltway was that Porter should, under no circumstances, appoint a replacement. Zackery's death marked only the fourth time in seventy years that a Supreme Court Justice had died in office. The previous one was that of Bostyn Dodge, Harvard law school grad, and former Harvard Law Review editor.

Zackery's death was also the seventh occasion since 1900 in which a seat on the Supreme Court of the United States was vacant during a year in which a presidential election was set to occur.

※

WARD ADAIR WAS NOT A HANDSOME MAN. THE MUCH RESPECTED political operative and campaign manager had blotchy skin, intense, narrow, dark eyes, and stood only 5 feet 8 inches. He was, however, fighting fit with buzzed cut white blond hair. He had a reputation for being blunt, calculating and usually right. At 45, the man wasn't well liked but was highly respected by everyone who had ever worked with him.

Adair stood as the President and First Lady entered the same sitting room where the pair had previously met with Oklahoma oil man Alder Mathers and his *"gang of four."* A woman rose with Adair. She was as bubbly as her partner was stoic. He offered his hand but not a smile.

"Mr. President. Mrs. Randall. This is my wife, Ella Suzuki."

The beaming lady of 43 years, dressed in a pink suit and flashing beautiful white teeth, shook hands with the First Couple, too.

"Welcome," Deidra said.

"Thank you for seeing us," Ella said.

"The pleasure is ours," Porter said taking her hand for a moment and then gesturing for everyone to sit.

It was evident to Deidra that Ella both admired and loved her husband. There was an undeniable current that connected the political pair. Although polar opposites in many ways, they were a couple, united and strong.

"Mr. President, we all know why we're here. Shall we cut to the chase?"

"I think we need to talk a little first. We have agreed to run, but we don't want to be part of any traditional political campaign."

"So we've been told," Ward Adair said glancing at his wife.

"And that's part of the reason I'm here," she said. "Ward and I have never worked together — in fact, we're usually on opposite sides politically. This will be the first time we're on the same team."

"And we are honored," Porter said. "We are aware of your professional pedigrees and acknowledge that we are total novices at this."

"Which can be very much to our advantage," Ella Suzuki smiled. "You're not wanting to use dirty tricks is such a refreshing approach — I can't express how unique that is."

"Is it naive or stupid?" Porter asked.

"I don't know that we should characterize it —," Ella began but she was cut off by her husband.

"Both, I'd say. Forty — sixty, maybe." Ward was known to be blunt and even combative.

"And can you work with that?" Porter asked without a pause.

"Of course," Ella began but she was again interrupted before she could say anything more.

"If those are your ground rules, we'll have to work that way."

"Have you ever done it — or even considered it before?"

"Mr. President, every candidate is different — every campaign has its own challenges," Ward said. "I will say that it will make for an interesting field test — but we're willing to take it on."

"Do you think it's possible to win with such an approach?"

"It's never been tried before, Mr. President."

"But if anyone can do it," Ella said, "Ward and I are the ones to pull it off."

"You are going to work together?" Deidra asked.

"We are. That will be a new experience for us — one we're looking forward to."

"I'm glad," Deidra said.

"Let's understand what we're up against," Ward said. "First, only Teddy Roosevelt has gone to the White House unelected and then won reelection to the office. When he tried to run as a third party candidate, he failed. All attempts to run as a third party have crashed and burned.

"That's just history. But there are also the organizations, funding, and total infrastructure of an established political party. We don't have any worries in the funding department. But the organization, nationally and state by state, is a tremendous challenge. With the help of social media, we can overcome a great deal — and we will. But we all need to understand where we stand and how big this rock is we're going to try and push up this hill.

"The Republicans should know their history. James K. Polk is the only President to have served as Speaker of the House before being elected President.

"Rutherford B. Hayes is one of five Presidents to lose the popular vote but win the office. He won the election by one electoral vote.

"George Bush, 43, was the first sitting Vice President to be elected President since Martin Van Buren."

"Where does that put us? What do we do first?" Porter asked.

"No unelected President has ever been elected to succeed himself. If we pull this off, you'll be the first."

"First off you'll need a VP," Ella Suzuki said. "Anyone in mind?"

Porter said, "I had thought about Greg Montgomery." The jovial Tea Party Senator from South Dakota, was well known and well thought of.

"We could work with him," Adair said with a glance to Ella.

But Porter and Deidra looked at each other and after a moment they both said, "Tracy Holyoak."

Both Ward Adair and his wife knew the former 3 term Libertarian representative from Wyoming. She was a former prosecutor who sat on the House Oversite Committee. She was known as a combative but highly principled government critic who was down to earth. She had left politics in despair after losing many Congressional fights during Porter's first term. The pair of political campaign operatives didn't know that Holyoak and Porter had become friends before he left Congress and had stayed in touch ever since.

Adair and Suzuki raised their eye brows to each other in approval.

"Excellent," he said. "She still has many admirers."

"And strong favorability numbers," Ella added.

"Do you think she will run?" Ward asked.

"I know," Porter said, "that she's been less satisfied back home as a county prosecutor than she had hoped. All we can do is ask."

"Call her and if she's on board, you'll need to make an official announcement — the sooner the better. Your *coming out* will trigger several items in the election law. But at this point we'll need every minute to get things in a row."

"If she's willing, she could fly in tomorrow and we could make an announcement then." Porter said looking over to Deidra who nodded in agreement.

"Are there people in the White House you'll need to inform first?" Ella asked.

"People who won't leak it." Ward said.

"I think so."

"Then we need to get to work on a stump speech. Think about why you're running and what you want to accomplish. This needs to be a speech that the media will pick a slice here and a slice there — different sound bites — to make each campaign event seem unique as they report them."

"I have some excellent speech writers already," Porter said.

"But they're officially working for you in the White House. We'll need to make some decisions because there are things which, by law, need to be completely separate. Some of your White House people may need to quit in order to join the campaign. They can come back to the White House after the race — assuming we win."

"We will win!" Ella said. "None of us are into this to lose."

"Make the call, Mr. President."

CHAPTER 6

Deidra sat in a chair beside the Resolute Desk in the Presidential Study next to the Oval Office. Porter pressed the speaker button on his desk phone. His Secretary, Gwendolyn Jacobs, told them through the intercom that Mrs. Holyoak was on the line.

"Tracy," Porter said.

"Mr. President," came her cheerful sounding voice.

"Hi, Tracy," Deidra said.

"Deidra? To what do I owe this pleasure — or am I speaking too soon?"

They all shared a chuckle.

"We do have a proposition for you," Porter said.

"You know I'm a very happily married woman, don't you?"

"Of course. Has Bradley recovered from losing State by that one field goal?"

"Oh, yes. He has learned to shake it off — just like he teaches his teams. He's about to start one-a-day drills with this year's squad."

"Good for him. How about you? Any more pleased with what you're doing?"

"It's about the best I can do until something better comes up.

What surprises me is how many drug crimes I've been prosecuting. But it's better than trying to deal with a dysfunctional Congress."

"Maybe we *do* have a better offer," Deidra said.

"Give me your best shot."

Porter took a breath before he began.

"A very unusual and unexpected set of circumstances has presented itself."

"With you, Porter, I wouldn't think unusual circumstance would be anything new."

"Good point. Well, you're aware then Tossen and the Democrats as well as the Sturges/Rifkin team for the Republicans have totally avoided the amendments proposals?"

"Yes. I was hoping for better from Sturges."

"Well, it's not happening."

"Okay, so?"

"I'm going to throw my Stetson into the ring of fire."

"Really? I was hoping you'd do that. So you'er going to be an Independent?"

"Yes. And with all the baggage that entails."

"You've got my support, Porter. One hundred and ten percent."

"I'd like to ask more than that. I need a running mate."

There was silence on the line for several seconds. Finally Tracy Holyoak spoke.

"My first reaction is — yes. But you know I've got to talk this over with Bradley."

"Without question," Deidra said. "But things are moving very fast here and the people who are behind all this, meaning our campaign team of Adair and Suzuki, wants Porter to announce ASAP."

"And I'd like for you to be here when we do announce," Porter said.

"Understood. Okay, I know Bradley is going to be all for this — even before I ask him. So, let's say we fly in. Tonight."

"Great," Porter said. "We could tell the staff here tomorrow and spring it on the media at the 2 o'clock press briefing."

"It'll make a hell of a story."

"That's what we're hoping for."

"Unless you hear differently from me within the hour, count me in. And we'll both be on the red eye into Dullas."

"I'll have a car waiting for you. And I'll put you two up in the Lincoln Bedroom."

"How could I turn that offer down?" Tracy laughed.

※

THE NEXT MORNING, TRACY AND BRADLEY HOLYOAK HAD breakfast with the First Couple.

"You two look bright eyed," Porter said.

"That's what a little Clear Eye — and a roll in a national historical site will do for you," Tracy grinned.

"I told you," Deidra winked at Porter.

"Did you two have a bet on us?" Bradley said. He was an athletic looking man with blue eyes and a perpetual suntan.

"No bet," Porter said.

"But it's what we would have done, too," Deidra shrugged.

"God bless America," Tracy said and they all laughed.

When the four got down to discussing specifics, there was no disagreement with Porter's campaign plans. In fact, Tracy beamed at the idea of no dirty tricks.

"What about all the history against a third party run?" Tracy asked.

"I'm hoping we will make history by becoming the exception."

"Ambitious," Bradley said.

"We're not going into this blindly," Porter said. "And neither are our campaign managers. It's going to take a hell of an effort — but I think we have the team to at least make it possible."

"How did you get Ward Adair and Ella Suzuki to work together?" Tracy wanted to know. "I know they're married but don't they usually work against each other?"

"That's their pattern," Deidra said. "But they seem to be pleased to be on the same side for once."

"I'll bet. I never understood how they could stay together while being on such opposite sides politically."

"I'm sure it has a lot to do with the Gang of Four?" Porter said.

"I bed your pardon?" Tracy put her coffee cup down with a clatter.

"Alder Mathers, Alice Niesson, Deacon Vaughn, and Elliot Mara. They're the ones who set up the exploratory committee and procured Adair and Suzuki. Although that's not the right word. Let's say, '... acquired the services of....'"

"Well, I'm impressed. What do the Gang of Four want?"

"Only for me to run. And your name was on top of their list of running mates."

"What else?"

"Nothing."

"They said we wouldn't hear from them again," Deidra said. "They didn't suggest any policies or directions. I think the amendments were their main priority."

"Then we are on the same page," Tracy said.

CHAPTER 7

Porter called a 1 PM meeting of selected staff in the Oval Office. Deidra was there along with Chief-of-Staff Graham Newcome and brother-in-law Mark Meehan, husband to Porter's sister, Irene, a retired NASA rocket scientist. Others in the room were Cinnamon Higdon, Director of White House Communications, president's speech writer, Therese Herzog, and Vice President Sundee Ives. When everyone was gathered, Porter used the intercom to ask Presidential Secretary, Gwendolyn Jacobs, to come join the group.

Everyone knew Tracy Holyoak but had no idea what was going on. When everyone was seated on either one of the two facing couches in the conversation area or in chairs in front of the fireplace, Porter spoke.

"In a few minutes I'm going to make an announcement at the Press Briefing that I've decided to run for President as an Independent. Mrs. Holyoak will be my running mate."

Porter let these words sink in before he said anything else.

When he did speak, he said, "The main reason for this run isn't because I want to be President as much as I want the Constitutional Amendments we've offered to be on the ballot. The only way to insure that happens is for me to be on the ballot, too. It's as plain and simple as that. Whatever you might think, that's it."

There were murmurs in the room and people exchanged a few words, but no one spoke up for all to hear. So, Porter went on.

"I want to keep the White House and the campaign separate — well as separate as possible. Anything done for the campaign is to be reported as such and billed appropriately. I understand that it will change many of the dynamics here — but I want you all to know that my prime focus is still doing this job — and you all know how important you are to accomplishing that. I'm just the figurehead in many ways, but it's you people who make this Executive Branch work. I'd like for you to keep doing that."

Looking around the room, even Porter didn't notice the furtive glances his Chief-of-Staff couldn't keep himself from making at Cinnamon. Graham sighed and turned his attention back to the President.

After another pause, Porter continued, "I know most of you have special relationships with particular reporters — but I'm asking you to give me the next half hour to make the announcement before you let any of this out. Please."

※

THE PRESS ROOM OF THE WEST WING, THE JAMES S. BRADY PRESS Briefing Room, sits over what was once the White House swimming pool. It was built with private donations for FDR in 1933.

When the space was still a pool, it featured underwater lighting, sterilizers and the latest gadgets to aid the handicapped President. Later, Truman swam in it often — with his glasses on. In 1961 a huge mural was painted by Bernard Lamotte occupying three walls of the space for President Kennedy. The painting was a gift from the President's father. It featured a Caribbean scene with many sailboats on calm waters. The opposite long wall was fitted with mirrors.

During the Johnson administration, the walls were hung with dozens of bathing suits of all sizes so that guests could swim.

It was President Nixon who turned the space into a press room. A wooden floor was built over the pool. The doors opened to the Rose

Garden on the south and the West Wing drive on the north. This allowed the members of the media quick access to outdoor events.

In the early 1980s, the Reagan administration remodeled the room, giving it the theater seats and blue decor it has had since then. In 2005 the oval backdrop reading, "The White House - Washington," was first hung behind the podium on the curtains. The space now has 48 small theater-style chairs that are crammed together only feet from the podium where Press Secretaries hold court Mondays through Fridays at 1 PM Eastern time. Video and still cameras, ladders and other equipment are piled along two walls and in the back of the room.

This was the room Porter entered at precisely 1 PM. The surprised media quickly got to their feet as the President held up a hand and said, "Thank you. Please take your seats."

"First things first," he said as soon as the reporters were seated and the cameras were focused on him. "The death of a second chief justice on my watch has been the subject of much debate and speculation. I want to clear that up as much as possible. Tomorrow I will be submitting to the Senate the name of current Associate Justice Isabel Greycore to be the new Chief Justice of the Supreme Court. This has the backing of the sitting Justices and makes sense. First of all because the court needs a Chief Justice to do its business. Secondly, instead of my nominating a new outside person to fill that position — as has usually happened in the past at the death of the Chief Justice — a current Justice understands what the court needs much more than someone new could possibly know. This was my practice after the passing of Chief Justice David Fish. Also, by doing this and expecting a quick confirmation process, I will NOT be nominating another Associate Justice. That position will remain open."

Porter took a breath before saying, "I'll take a few questions."

The President indicated Buzz Yeager, the INK White House middle-aged correspondent who wore his tortoise shelled bifocals parked an inch into his thinning brown hair.

"You are abiding by the Biden Rule, then, Mr. President?"

Among the photo journalists in that Briefing Room was White House Photographer, Leigh Janda. He was documenting the event as he had in the closed door Oval Office meeting before this press conference. The associate professor of photojournalism, squat, 40's with a fringe of remaining blond hair around the edges of his head, was on an extended leave of absence from Northwestern University's McDill School of Journalism. He knew that his pictures would one day be a source of historical record for the Randall years in the White House. Janda used a Nikon D4 digital single lens reflex camera to memorialize the moments.

"There is no 'Biden Rule,'" Porter responded. "There never was. Biden proposed the rule when he was chair of the Senate Judiciary Committee — but it was never accepted by either his committee, the Senate, nor even of the Democratic party who supported it at the time. If you'll recall, then Senator Biden in '92 was trying to prevent then President Bush 41 from appointing another member to the court after the contentious nomination of Clarence Thomas. At the time there was actually no vacancy to fill. But it was a very volatile political season and the Democrats had hopes of unseating the senior Bush — which they ultimately did and replaced him with Bill Clinton.

"However no one had ratified the so-called 'Biden Rule' then or since. As a point in fact, it was the Democrats, President Obama who first abandoned the idea when Merit Garland was nominated in 2016 — an election year. And Obama's Vice President was Joe Biden. It will be interesting to see how many of you just happen to leave that fact out of your reports today."

Porter pointed to WOLF Cable Network's Demona Enock, the strawberry blonde in the choker-collared knit dress with a diamond shaped cut out between the collar and her cleavage.

"Mr. President, if you're not following the 'Biden Rule,' what are you doing?"

"Doing the right thing. I'm not trying to set any precedent on my own. But because of the way I came to office and because of the little time left on that clock, I simply think it's not a good idea for an unelected occupant of this office to attempt to reshape or restructure the Supreme Court. That job should be left to the next elected President."

Next Porter called on the Associate Press correspondent, Doy Urbie, 40's, of middle eastern extraction with dark sand colored skin and close cropped black hair. Urbie was well respected by his colleagues and was considered one of the sharpest and well connected members of the White House Press Corps.

"Since Justice Greycore has already been through the nomination process under President Gibson, do you expect any hesitation or delay in considering her elevation to Chief Justice?"

"Not at all. Justice Greycore is well respected and is the choice of her colleagues on the court for this position; I expect this to be a virtual shoo-in."

The other questions were light weight and of little substance. Finally the President said, "If there are no more questions about this subject, let's move on to the chief reason I'm here."

※

Tracy and Bradley Holyoak had sneaked into the Press Room unnoticed while Porter was answering questions. When Porter turned to Tracy, he said, "I'd like former Representative Tracy Holyoak to join me here."

Tracy stood and stepped up beside Porter.

"Today I am officially announcing that I am running for the office of President of the United States."

Reporters were scribbling notes and checking the time on their watches and phones.

"Mrs. Tracy Holyoak has agreed to be my Vice Presidential running mate. We are running as Independents. The reason for this run is not ambition on either of our parts for the respective positions nor for the power of these offices. We are running to shine the spotlight of public scrutiny on the two Constitutional Amendments I've proposed — the Congressional Term Limits and the Balanced Budget Amendments. Both have the needed signatures to be on the ballots in all 50 states and territories. We all know they will never pass in Congress. In the past two years they have never been voted out of committee. We don't see that status changing. Mrs. Holyoak and I want these amendments to have a chance to be voted on by the public and become law the only way possible. Our run is going to be tied to these two proposals. That is our goal. Period.

"We are fully aware that history and political pundit thinking is against it. For that reason I think we might well use the song from Smokey and the Bandit as our theme. 'We have a long way to go and a short time to get there. We're going to do what they say can't be done.' We'll see.

"Now, I want to let you hear from Mrs. Holyoak. Tracy." Porter stepped back as he pressed a button under the lip of the podium. A one step platform slid out from the bottom, and the Vice Presidential candidate, all 4 feet 11 inches of her, stepped up and addressed the reporters.

"No *short people got no reason to live* jokes, please," she said referring to the Randy Newman song. "My reason to live right now is these two amendments. President Randall and I are on the same page. This is not about us. It's about these amendments — which polls indicate have the support of the American public. But they would put an end to the good life as Congress has known it for a long time. That way of living and not truly addressing the needs of the public was my reason for leaving Congress four years ago. This race, and the amendments we stand for, is the reason I've come back.

"We have all watched with admiration and respect at the job President Randall has done since the death of President Gibson. We're all in a much better place now than we were before fate thrust him into the highest office in the land. It is my honor to stand beside him and to make this run together."

Tracy started to step down, but Porter caught her with a hand at her back and urged her to stay where she was. He stepped up beside the podium and moved the twin microphones so they were half way between them.

"A few questions," Porter said.

"How long has this been in the works?" Abner Moss, another liberal TV cable news reporter famous for his ambush style and his *got 'ya* questions, was the first with a question.

"Not that long. You know there was an exploratory committee formed before either of the conventions."

"So, you were thinking about it then?" Oblivious to his patently bad comb-over, the red faced journalist squinted his small dark eyes.

"It was under consideration."

"Didn't the Republicans offer you the top spot on their ticket?"

"The Republicans have chosen Vincent Sturges and Trey Rifkin. It's been all over the news," Porter answered before pointing to the Associate Press's Doy Urbie. He looked down at the question he had written on his reporter's note pad.

"Is it true that Ward Adair and Ella Suzuki are running your campaign — together?" the man with dark sand colored skin and close cropped black hair asked.

"Yes," Porter said. "And it's a real coup to have them." Porter turned to WOLF Cable Network's Demona Enock.

The strawberry blonde asked, "When will you two begin campaigning together?"

Tracy leaned in and said, "We just started."

There was a light chuckle from the reporters.

Tracy talked over the crowd saying, "We don't have a schedule worked out — but we will very soon and we'll let you all know when we do."

Porter pointed to Buzz Yeager, the middle aged INK White House reporter. Yeager had pulled his bifocals down from his thinning brown hair and had glasses perched on the end of his nose.

"If you win, Mr. President, will you again forgo your salary?"

"Good question, Buzz. No, I won't — because I can't. I'm nowhere as rich as some of the people who have occupied this office before. I was happy to make the gesture these last two years, but I can't afford to do that anymore. Like most Americans, I need to be paid for the work I do. Even if my next novel happens to be a success, I can't afford to do this job for free without going in the red. Congress seems to think going in the red is all right for the country, but I don't subscribe to that way of thinking for anyone or any business. And government is a business — one without any tangible product to sell. The only money the government has is the taxpayers' money. And anyone who believes that the government can provide *anything* for free isn't connecting the dots. It's free for Congress to legislate anything it likes because the money to pay for it doesn't come out of their pockets. Nothing is really free to the average citizen. *'Single payer'* or 'free from the government" --- it's you who end up paying for it.

"One way you can look at this campaign is that Tracy and I are applying for jobs. We expect to be paid if we're hired, but we don't feel the need to be compensated beyond any tenure we have in office. When we step down, we don't expect to keep getting our salaries for the rest of our lives. Nobody should. It's just plain wrong. But the way things are now, the President, the Vice President, the members of the Supreme Court, and members of Congress, even if they have only served a single term, are compensated as long as they live. That's not what we're seeking."

CHAPTER 8

"Somebody has access to what we're writing."

Saundra stood in Howard's study in his penthouse, an angry expression on her face.

"Who? How?" Howard wanted to know. "And how do you know?"

"Look at these." She handed him two dozen printout pages from the Internet. "These are from Chapter 3 and 4. Both have my additions and corrections. But I'm not sending them to anyone. But someone has access to them — through me."

Howard looked over the sheets and asked, "Does our publisher have a connection to one of our computers?"

"Absolutely not. Everything I write is saved to a flash drive and I bring it to you. I'm not taking the chance of sending it to the cloud or over the Internet in any fashion."

"Then how is it getting out there?"

"I have a computer security gal coming over to my place this afternoon. We'll find out. If we can't find the problem at my place, I'll bring her over here."

"Okay," Howard said sitting back in his chair. "But this doesn't make any sense."

"It's the kind of thing I wouldn't put past Zeb Tolle. If Watergate hadn't happened before his time, I'd suspect him of being one of the *'plumbers'*. He loves that kind of crap."

"Okay. Here's my next chapter," Howard said offering her both printed pages and a flash drive.

MCKINNA MCPHEE WAS A 31 YEAR-OLD COMPUTER SECURITY wizard. Saundra had engaged her as a resource on several news stories over the years. The slender woman always wore a dark slacks suit and white silk blouse under her jacket. Besides her wedding ring, the only jewelry she wore was a small gold St. George's cross. She had brown hair which hung to her shoulders with premature gray streaks. She used her long fingers with plain nail polish to explore the configuration of Saundra's computer.

When she had finished her software and hardware detective work, she turned to Saundra who stood behind her trying to understand what might have been found. "What is your routine with the material you bring in from Howard?"

"I take the flash drive we've exchanged and plug it into my machine. I open up his file in MS Word and begin editing it using the Review tab."

"And when you're done?"

"I print out a copy. Howard would rather read a printed page than a computer screen."

McPhee turned back to the flat screen monitor. After a moment of looking she turned around and found the printer on the cadenza behind the desk. She got up from the desk and stepped over to the printer. She examined it, picking it up and reading the tag on the back.

Next she went to the window which looked out on another apartment building fifty yards away. Typical of New York apartments, both had open curtains.

"Do you know your neighbors?"

"In New York?" Saundra laughed. "I know the people on both sides of me and the lady above. There's somebody new below me — and I have no idea who lives across the way."

"How long ago did these new tenants move in?"

"Within this past week."

"Right around the time you started having problems."

"Yes, why —?"

Mckinna McPhee made a face and bit down on her lower lip before she sat down across from Saundra's desk.

"Here's what I think is happening. When you print, you're not hardwired to your printer. You're sending your material via Bluetooth."

"So?"

"Bluetooth printers are usually Class 2 devices. They have a range of about 10 meters or 33 feet. Yours is a high end printer and is a Class 1. It has a range of 100 meters or 328 feet."

"I wanted to be able to print from a laptop even in the living room."

"Oh, I get it. But with that kind of range, even though concrete flooring, your printer signal can be picked up by any of the connected apartments. They could even add a range extender or signal booster to improve the quality. Then the signal could be picked up by another computer — and they could do whatever they liked with what they picked up."

Saundra sagged into her desk chair.

"What do I do?"

"I'd connect your printer with a cable. Use a carpet strip to cover it up so you don't ruin it by walking on it. I can reset your computer preferences so it will only use the hard wire and not Bluetooth. And I wouldn't try to print from your laptop."

"Is there nothing I can do to whoever is stealing my signal?"

"When it's in the air, it's open to the public."

"Damn," Saundra said.

"And you should check your home security. Anybody who is willing to do this, might be willing to try to get into your computer physically."

"All right. Do you think you should check Howard's system?"

"If we're going to do this right, we need to do that, too."

Howard's penthouse was in good shape security wise. The only Bluetooth he used was for his mouse. Everything else was hard wired.

He enjoyed meeting Mckinna McPhee, whom he'd talked with over the phone several times over the years.

"For what it's worth," she said, "we miss having you on the air."

"Thank you," Howard said. "But the only constant in this life is change."

"Don't I know it," she smiled.

"Mckinna believes I could have been hacked through my Bluetooth connection to my printer," Saundra said. "Since everything that showed up online was from my printouts that I brought to you, we think we've fixed the problem."

"We should go back and examine those chapters."

"I already have some changes in mind. And I think we should include somewhere that the earlier draft was compromised. It'd be a good warning to the public."

"I like it," Howard said. Then to Mckinna he said, "I'd like you to come back and recheck everything in a couple of weeks."

"I was going to suggest the same thing," she said.

"We thought we were being security conscious by only exchanging hard copies and flash drive text."

"Good idea," Mckinna said. "But these days you can never be too careful. And now that you know someone is trying to get copies of your material, nothing you do can be too safe."

"Got it," Howard said and Saundra agreed.

"I was just thinking," Saundra continued, "maybe we should include something about computer security in the book — beyond what we've experience. We know all journalists have or will have to deal with this."

"There's something I've not considered," Howard said. "Mckinna, are you willing to be our resource for that?"

"Of course. More than happy to help."

"It would also be worth looking into journalists who have been hacked," Howard said.

"I'll look into that," Saundra said.

"I can think of the Robert Muller Trump/Russia probe, Watergate, and the Daniel Elsworth psychiatrist's notes being stolen. That's hacking before computers."

"I see a new chapter here," Saundra said typing herself notes into her smart phone.

CHAPTER 9

As the campaigns rolled on, both the Democrats and the Republicans attacked Porter and Tracy. Their primary thrust was that Porter had said he didn't want the job and wasn't going to run for another term. After two days the Republicans revealed they had offered the chance for Porter to run on their ticket but he didn't accept it.

Pundits in print, on the air, and on cable were claiming that the new entry would hurt the Republicans. An Independent would siphon potential votes from the GOP more than from the Democrats, it was claimed. The media generally celebrated this fact by claiming the move was, in effect, handing victory to the George Tossen/Amelia Morris Democrat ticket.

An amusing storm erupted on Twitter pointing out that Porter had gotten the lyrics wrong to the Smokey and the Bandit theme song. The line, "We're going to do what they say can't be done" came before the "We have a long way to go and a short time to get there."

Ward Adair and Ella Suzuki both were thrilled with the movie and the song reference. Ward had a cartoon drawn up with a Burt-Reynolds-looking Porter beside a Sally-Fields-appearing Tracy. They were seated in a T-bar, black Pontiac Trans AM flying down the road.

The caption read, "We're going to do what they say can't be done." The song was also put in as the campaign theme song, playing just before Porter or Tracy took to the stage on any political rallies.

What surprised everyone were the size and the enthusiasm that awaited them each time they spoke. At first Porter and Tracy were side by side in Houston, Dallas, and Kansas City. The overflow crowds made the campaign began booking larger venues for the pair's appearances.

※

THE RALLY IN ANN ARBOR, MICHIGAN, SHOWED THE GROWING support for the Independent ticket. The University Baseball Field was packed with 13,000 cheering supporters. It became difficult for the media to downplay what was quickly becoming a wave of public support.

When Porter took to the stage, the Smokey and the Bandit theme blared from speakers. The audience was on their feet singing along. The stage shook. The platform had been erected in the outfield to allow for the diamond and most of the infield to be covered with folding chairs. The applause ran for three minutes before Porter could speak.

"What a welcome, Michigan!" he said and the crowd thundered for another full minute.

"Ronald Reagan liked to tell the story from the old Soviet Union about a fellow who wanted to buy a car. In the Soviet Union, under their system, if you wanted to buy a car, you had to pay for it up front and then wait 10 years to get your car. The story was that one man had paid his money and the car dealer told him, 'Okay, come back in 10 years and pick up your car.' And the man said, 'Morning or afternoon?' The car dealer said, 'It's 10 years from now. What difference does it make?' Then the man said, "Well, the plumber is coming in the morning."

The crowd erupted in laughter.

"This was a Soviet example of what Reagan like to say about our system — that the 9 most terrifying words in the English language were, 'I'm from the government and I'm here to help.'"

Again the crowd roared.

"Here and now under our system, too many people are looking to the government for help and solutions. What they don't realize is that it's the government that's the problem."

This brought cheers and applause.

"When our forefathers designed our 'One nation under God, with Liberty and Justice for all' — the Constitutional system of '...government of the people, by the people, and for the people...' they knew that the system that governs least governs best.

"Somewhere along the way we've lost sight of that. We've become addicted and dependent on government. Where did that come from? When did it become the American dream to live off the government? Remember that the government doesn't have any money. The government doesn't do ANYTHING that makes a profit. The only money the government has is *your* money."

The crowd didn't like the sound of that and their grumbling was significant.

"The way the government gets your money is by taxing you — requiring you to pay for things you wouldn't fund if you had a choice. But government doesn't ask you. Congress passes bills and taxes your gasoline, your food, your drinks, your house, your car, and anything you buy. In a way, it is punishment for doing well — because the better you do in this life, the more taxes you pay — and you pay for people who don't work — and those who simply don't *want* to work. How is that fair? I don't think so."

Applause and agreement came from the crowd.

"What happened to the rugged individual — the American who didn't want anybody's help — like our parents and grandparents who took pride in doing for themselves — but were happy to help those who needed it? They were the worker bees, the worker ants and not the lazy grasshoppers. They took responsibility for their lives and their choices — and held their heads high for doing it.

"That's the America I grew up in and the one I'd like to see again.

"That's why Tracy Holyoak and I are running for office. We want to help put America back on the right path — the path to responsibility and good government.

"The two Constitutional Amendments we support will go a long way to helping us achieve what we're after. We are here asking for your help and support. Do you want what we want?"

The crowd detonated into cheers and thunderous applause.

When Porter could speak over the roar again, he said, "I want you to hear from Tracy. She was in Congress and you remember how she fought against corruption then. She's helping me do it again now."

Porter turned and gestured for Tracy to step forward.

※

TRACY RAISED HER HANDS TO THE CROWD WHILE AN AID PUT A platform in place behind the podium. She stepped up on it and adjusted the microphones.

"Like I told the press, I don't want to hear any of those *short people* jokes. Short people know we're short — but we also know how to kick shins and punch other things that can really get your attention."

The crowd loved it.

"The point of Congress is to represent the people of this nation. But today over half the members of Congress are millionaires. Of the 534 current members of the House and Senate, 268 had an average net worth of $1 million. That's 12 times richer than the average American household. And Congress seems to be very concerned about income inequality among the rest of us. Do you think they're the best ones to represent us? Do you really think they are representing you?

"No," came the shout from the crowd.

"Most of them weren't millionaires when they came to Washington. So how did they get that rich on government salaries? Did they all win the lottery and just forgot to tell the rest of us? Or is there something rotten in the Washington, DC zip code?"

The response was guttural from the crowd.

"How did the zip codes in and around DC get to be some of the wealthiest in the nation?"

The murmuring from the audience said it all.

"Do you believe a Congressional Term amendment will ever get out of the House Governmental Affairs Committee or the Senate Oversight Committee? No, I don't either.

"Serving in Congress should be an honor, not a career. The Founding Fathers envisioned citizen legislators — people who would serve their term or terms, then go home and back to work.

"Here's what the Term Limits Amendment says. There are 8 points. Number one: Term Limits. Members of Congress shall serve no more than a total of 12 years consecutively or in total. Two six-year terms for the Senate or six two-year terms for the House of Representatives.

Number 2: There is no tenure and no pension. Members of Congress are to be paid for the time they serve. A member of either house of Congress may collect a salary while in office but receives no pay or benefits when they are out of office.

3. Congress — past, present & future — participates in Social Security. All funds in the Congressional retirement fund move to the Social Security system immediately. All future funds flow into the Social Security system, and Congress participates with the American people.

4. Congress can purchase their own retirement plan, just as all Americans do.

5. Congress loses their current health care system and participates in the same health care system as the American people.

6. Congress will no longer vote themselves a pay raise. Congressional pay is hereby tied irrevocably at the current level to the nation's Gross Domestic Product, overall Military pay, and the Social Security pay rate.

7. Congress must equally abide by all laws they impose on the American people.

8. All contracts with past and present Congress members are void effective the first day of January after this Amendment becomes law.

9. In the event of any, partial or complete, government shut down — for any reason whatsoever — the pay for members of Congress and their staff will be held until the government is completely reopened.

10. After completing their elected and lawful government terms in

office, members of Congress are hereby to be ostracized from Washington, D.C., meaning they may not live in nor work in-or-around the nation's capital for the next decade. They may not work for any public or private company specializing in their field of service during this term either.

The American people did not make the current contract with Congressmen. Congressmen made all these contracts for themselves.

CHAPTER 10

When Porter and Tracy first announced their campaign, the media treated it as a joke. Some pundits accused Porter of reneging on his former claim neither to desire the power and prestige of the presidency— nor to ever run for it. Since most of the outlets were primarily left leaning, they gave the third party ticket little attention believing it was going to harm the Republicans more than the Democrats.

For their part the Democrats were of the same mind and did little things to encourage the Independents. But after Porter and Tracy began their first campaign swing the polls showed that in fact they were drawing as much from the left as from the right. Although the Randall/Holyoak ticket was only drawing a few thousand attendees in Texas up to Michigan, the brain trusts behind the scene at Democratic Party headquarters decided it was not such a good strategy to just ignore the pair. Their opposition research teams began looking into ways to discredit or weaken the Indy challenge.

A former Afghan P.O.W. got in touch with an N.B.C. reporter with the claim that Porter had tried to kill him when he was brought into an operating tent in Helmand Province. The story was forwarded to the Tossen/Morris campaign where it found fertile soil.

Over two weeks after the story was first floated, it appeared as a new story on the network's nightly newscast and on all its affiliate networks. A filmed interview with the former Taliban fighter told the story in Farsi with English subtitle translation. According to the then POW. and the translation, he was wounded in both legs and evacuated to a US Army combat support hospital, called a C-H-S, "cash," where he was to be operated on. Still conscious, the fighter was secured to a stretcher and carried into the tent operating theater. No sooner was he on the table than the surgeon, later revealed to be Major Porter Randall, brought about the event. The doctor, according to the POW grabbed the pistol out of the holster of an Army M.P/medic at the foot of the litter and fired it across the body of the terrified soldier. There was oxygen in the tent which could have exploded and the move was designed to frighten the already traumatized man. However, the soldier didn't react but held his tongue — expecting to die in enemy hands at any moment.

The resulting news story was carried in multiple on-line newspapers. The headline was, "President Was A Reckless Doctor In Afghanistan" and "President Participated In US Torture."

The story took over cable news and became the topic of evisceration by talking heads wanting to discredit and damage the President as a stable, reliable leader.

While the story raged, Porter and Tracy had parted company. He had returned to DC while she continued campaigning in Wisconsin, Minnesota, and a final welcoming home rally in Montana. She was unprepared to answer questions about the incident and instead continued to focus on the Constitutional Amendments on the ballot.

The next afternoon at the daily White House press briefing, Cinnamon Higdon, Director of White House Communications, had taken over the role of Press Secretary. The 35 year-old, five foot seven, African and Korean beauty with coal dark hair, and beautiful features, faced the press with her usual intelligence and intensity.

Before answering any question or even making an opening statement, she introduced a shorter woman who wore no make-up under her gray streaked shoulder length hair. She had pale blue eyes and an oval face. She wore the uniform of an Army officer with a single star on her shoulders.

"My name is Nara Follett. N-a-r-a — F-o-l-l-e-t. I am a Brigadier General and Chief of the Army Nurse Corp. My office is in the Pentagon. At the time of the alleged story about President Randall firing a pistol in an emergency OR in Afghanistan — I was a M5 - Emergency Nurse assigned to the CSH, or 'cash,' hospital in Helmand Province. I was standing right across from Major Randall when the shot was fired."

The press were delighted that the firing of a pistol in an operating tent had been confirmed. Many reporters were ready with how they were going to spin this report.

General Follet continued.

"What has not been reported was that an Afghan Sand Viper had crawled into the tent and was poised to strike me in the calf from behind. Major Randall did pull the pistol of the M.P./medic who was lifting one end of the stretcher onto the operating table. He shot the head off the snake. Major Randall then returned the pistol to the MP, asked to be re-gloved and continued with the medical procedure — which saved the Taliban soldier from having to have both of his legs amputated." She paused and then said, "Questions?"

"Did you know the snake was there?"

"No, not until after the major killed it."

"Were you shocked that a doctor would fire a weapon in an operating room?"

"Have you ever had a 9mm pistol fired right in front of you? Yes. It scared the hell out of me — but I was glad he did it. A nurse two weeks before almost lost her leg and her life to the same kind of snake just like that one."

"Wasn't that a violation of medical procedures?"

"There really aren't any rules or regulations to fit such an occasion. How could there be?"

"But you were shocked?"

"I was thankful."

"Was there any military disciplinary actions arising from the incident?"

"The major was recommended for a Bronze Star with V device for valor — but he declined it. He asked, 'What would anyone have done? It was just another day at the office.'"

WOLF News reported the next day that the story and its taped interview with the former Taliban fighter had come from Iraq through China. Other networks, including INK, were very slow to pick up on the story. When they did, they ran it with only brief coverage which was dropped after a couple of hours.

The Democrats abandoned their attacks as soon as the WOLF story surfaced. The Republican campaign, which was planning a major follow up blasting the President, quietly abandoned their efforts without saying a word.

CHAPTER 11

The next week both the Democrats and the Republicans opened a new attack on Porter and Tracy by claiming their campaign was an attack on the US Congress. Both camps took a different tact but it was obvious that somewhere along the line there had been a consensus to have a joint thrust. The Democrats used the phrase, "Attack on Congress" while the Republicans went with "Assault on Representative Government."

Slickly produced video ads for both appeared within hours of each other. They each hammered away at the theme that by putting the Constitutional Amendments on the state ballots, this was a ploy to skirt Congress in the amendment process.

The Randall/Holyoak campaign responded with an ad simply paraphrasing Article 5 of the Constitution — white letters over a purple background read by a voice-over announcer.

It read: "Whenever two thirds of both houses shall deem it necessary, the Congress of the United States shall propose amendments to this Constitution — or — (this part was highlighted in yellow) with the approval of the legislatures of two thirds of the several states, a convention for proposing amendments shall be called. Either case shall be valid. The Constitution, when ratified by the legislatures of three-fourths of the several states, or by conventions in three-fourths thereof, may be proposed by the Congress."

Both the Democrats and the Republicans howled that this ad distorted and misquoted the actual wording of the Constitution. It was a hot topic in the media, but it sputtered each time the words of the Constitution were placed side by side with the words of the Independent Party ad. To any observer it was evident that the ad was only a simplification and clarification of the precise legal text of the 5th Amendment.

The following week the campaign ran another ad quoting Article 10 of the Constitution. Again white letters over a purple background this one read, "The powers not delegated to the United States by the Constitution, nor prohibited by it to the States, are reserved to the States respectively, or to the people."

Try as they might neither party was able to refute nor counter this ad.

In the DC Offices of the Randall/Holyoak campaign, 5 feet 8 inch Ward Adair was thrilled with the way the war of words and ideas was playing out. His buzz cut white blond hair seemed to glow as he and wife, Ella Suzuki, encouraged their team in video conferences across the country. So far the Adair/Suzuki team had correctly predicted each turn in the campaign trail and was ready with carefully worded responses and edited clips of both the President and VP Candidate Tracy Holyoak with stirring music and flashy visuals. It was still going to be a long campaign but Adair and Suzuki knew their business and seemed to steer the perfect path.

The Democrats and the Republicans had to fall back on their much repeated claims of a war against Congress as their primary game plan.

HOWARD STERLING AND SAUNDRA FONTAN KEPT CRANKING OUT their Requiem for Journalism book chapter by chapter. Having fixed their security problem and being assured there were no more leaks, the pair was gaining speed and satisfaction with their work.

Their publisher was making arrangements with a small printer in

Nebraska to do the actual printing — all under a vail of total secrecy. The project had become the biggest and most cloaked project the publisher had ever undertaken. This was important because any more leakage of material from the book could prove disastrous.

The dirty tricks units of the established political parties were joining forces to produce bogus chapters in the hopes of damaging the prospects of the real book when it came out. INK was working on the project to be the prime vein for the misinformation. The problem shared by all was they no longer had access to the real manuscript and were blind as to what Howard and Saundra were really working on.

The fake material had to have some bites of truth in it in order to make it appear to be real. However, the questions were what kind of scandal could best discredit the book and by which party was it to be served up to that purpose. There was a real fear that if facts about a now forgotten misdeed were brought up, that it might reignite public fury over these past crimes.

What the joint dirty tricks team settled on were four scandals as their real basis. The thought was to tell a little of the truth first and then twist it as needed.

First was that of Tea Party leader, Henry Jude Radel for Florida. In 2013 he was caught in a cocaine sting. He was trying to buy 3.5 grams of a narcotic from undercover agents. Only 10 months into his first term in Congress, Radel, a former TV reporter and admitted alcoholic, was given one year probation and resigned from Congress.

This story pleased both the Democrats and the Republicans who always hated the Tea Party and the financial responsibility it stood for.

Next to be thrown under the bus of political expediency was the once popular Democratic former New York representative Anthony Weiner. The husband to long-time top aide to Hillary Clinton, Huma Abedin, Weiner was convicted of sending sexting pictures of his penis to three women. One of the recipients was 15 at the time. He used the internet name of Carlos Danger. Weiner's laptop was later found to have supposedly *"lost"* e-mails from then Presidential candidate Hillary Clinton.

The last ploy was the case of NSA whistleblower, Edward Snowden, known to be the most significant leaker of classified documents in

US history. Considered a neutral figure by the Democrats and the Republicans, the dirty tricks departments were eager to use his story as both fact and fiction. In an address via the Internet projected on large screens to students of Canada's Queen's University, Snowden said, "I don't live in Russia, I live on the Internet." Snowden's revelation that US security agencies were regularly spying on and collecting data on US citizens was a shock to the system of American justice. He escaped to Russia and knew he can't ever set foot in any nation with an extradition treaty with the US. His fear was capture and imprisonment if not death for charges of treason.

Here is where the deception began. Added to the Snowden tale was a totally unproven charge that he was a significant figure in Russia's attempts to influence American elections. Supposedly he had the most impact on the 2016 election of Donald Trump.

The supposedly leaked chapter of Howard and Saundra's manuscript dealt with the wasted funds of the IRS on pointless conferences, travel, and lavish parties. The new information offered by this twisted tale was that it was the Tea Party and the Independent party who were claiming to support such activities for *"special treatment."* What wasn't written about was the harassment, discrimination and useless document demands the IRS had made of the Tea Party while refusing them the same tax exempt status as those enjoyed by all other political parties.

Zeb Tolle at INK assigned writers who had worked for Howard and under Saundra to insure the verbiage and syntax of the "chapter" sounded like the writings and reporting of Howard and his producer.

When Howard and Saundra were questioned, they pointed out errors in their supposed chapters. The hoax was quickly debunked. But it only showed the growing fear that existed about what truths the pair would ultimately expose.

The TV ad called, "Hollywood Against Constitutional Change" hit the airwaves in one of the largest media buys of the campaign. It was late July when the ad appeared. A printed version went up on billboards and in full page ads in major city newspapers and news magazines.

The one minute spot featured actors and actresses, many academy award winners, in the costume and in character of their most memorable and powerful roles. The performers all were reading from the same script and the screen cut from one actor to the next sometimes in mid-sentence.

They began holding replicas of the Constitution and reading it in very solemn tones under dramatic lighting and moving music. Each performer only got a few words before the screen switched to the next.

"'We the People of the United States, / in order to form a more perfect Union, / establish Justice, / insure domestic Tranquility, / provide for the common defense, / promote the general Welfare, / and secure the Blessings of Liberty / to ourselves / and our Posterity, / do ordain and establish / this Constitution for the United States of America."

The actors then put down the Constitution and spoke to the camera, all reading from the same script which said:

"Changing our most basic founding document, / the Constitution of the United States / is nothing that should ever be taken lightly. / Our nation's founders laid out a process / by which their original work / could be altered / if needed /— and that process began with action / from our elected members of Congress. / It has always been done this way / — and done so carefully and with great thought.

"To attempt to corrupt / or pervert not just the process / but our very basic foundation as a nation / through untried and dangerous methods / should frighten us all / to the very core of our being.

"/ If changes need to be made, / we know the way it should be done. / Don't allow yourself to be misled / into taking us down a hazardous / and ill-advised path.

"/ Do not support / the proposed Constitutional changes / on our ballots. / Trust the process / we have always used.

Then all together the group shouted, "God bless America!"

CHAPTER 12

Porter was back in the White House that Saturday for his Fireside Chat. He was resurrecting the forum used by FDR. While Roosevelt used only radio, Porter was able to use video computer cameras and do both a Skype and a Mac Facetime chat.

This time he was in the Blue Room sitting beneath the portrait of George Washington that First Lady Dolly Madison has saved when the British burned the White House during the War of 1812.

Mrs. Madison, in a letter to her sister on the night of August 23, 1814, said a friend who came to help her escape was exasperated at the First Lady's insistence on saving the portrait. Yet, she was not be denied. The canvas was pulled out of its frame and rolled up. Two gentlemen from New York, she said, spirited it away for safe-keeping.

What Dolly Madison didn't know was that the portrait was actually a copy — not the original by Gilbert Stuart. The First Lady fled the White House and met her husband at a predetermined meeting place in the middle of a thunderstorm.

Sitting under that saved portrait, Porter spoke to his video audience.

"In case you've been living under a rock or hiding away somewhere to keep from being bothered, you know the presidential campaign season has begun. The Democrats have nominated Sen. George Tossen and Representative Amelia Morris as their standard bearers. The Republicans are offering two representatives, Vincent Sturges and Trey Rifkin.

"I've also decided to run and my running mate is former representative Tracy Holyoak. I've not changed my mind about really wanting this office, but our campaign is more about supporting the the two Constitutional Amendments, the 28th and the 29th — Congressional Term Limits and Balanced Budget.

"It wouldn't be fair for me to use *this* forum to promote my campaign — and I won't. This chat is about what's happening with your government that you need to know.

"My office has been in contact with the Israeli government for the last several weeks. We have been trying to work out a Mutual Defense Agreement. As you know, Israel alone is a functioning representative democratic republic in the Mid-East. We have been a supporter of that nation and its efforts to live in peace with its neighbors for years.

"It has reached a point where our alliance could be strengthened by a bi-lateral agreement to militarily support each other in the unlikely event of outside aggression. We have been offering Israel military equipment for their defense for many years and they have shared their advances in technology and medicine with us.

"We expect the cooperation to continue and grow even stronger in the years to come. What my office has decided is that a Mutual Defense Treaty, to be ratified by our Senate and the Israeli Knesset, would make two things very clear. First, it would show how intertwined our interests are and, secondly, how strongly we feel about supporting each other.

"The full text of the agreement is on line at WhiteHouse.gov. It will be available for your inspection and comment as it goes up to the Senate on Monday. Please feel free to give us your reactions and comments.

"On another matter," Porter said after taking a deep breath, "I have removed the Secret Service from direct control of Homeland Security and returned it to the Treasury Department. This organization has a long and stellar record there. By returning them to Treasury I am enabling the

Secret Service to continue its traditions. It will have its own budget and be able to recruit and train the most qualified men and women for its ranks. These will be those who appreciate what this fine organization has always stood for. They are to have a hand-in-glove relationship with Homeland Security. This is in no way a slap in the face for Homeland and the tremendous job they have and continue to do. The fact is that the Secret Service has gotten lost under the much larger organization. To be as effective as it once was, it needs to be nimble and much more focused.

"Lastly, I want to announce the Presidential Prizes for Creativity. John F. Kennedy once said, 'The American, by nature, is optimistic. He is experimental, an inventor and a builder who builds best when called upon to build greatly.'

"Next year on July 4th, whoever is President at that point, will award six $100,000 prizes. The categories are — writing — one for fiction and one for non-fiction — inventions — one each for mechanical, electrical, chemical and robotic — devices — tools or gadgets.

"The point of the Presidential Prizes for Creativity is to encourage American invention, discovery, and creativity."

WITHOUT PORTER OR TRACY'S KNOWLEDGE, WADE ADAIR AND Ella Suzuki arranged for counter TV, newspaper, news magazine, and billboard ads that were funded by an anonymous group with no affiliation to the Independent Party campaign.

This ad featured only one actor — Brian Edge. Edge was 51 years-old, and had been named the most handsome man in America over 6 times at different stages in his career. He had a rugged manliness about him with deep blue eyes, dark hair which was beginning to gray at his temples, and a voice that seemed to come almost from the center of the earth. He played both serious dramatic roles and light romantic comedies. He was still married to his high school sweetheart and now was an empty-nester with all his five children having become successful in their own rights.

Beyond the movies, Brian Edge was known for his tireless efforts to help vets, their families, and their children — usually anonymously — but word always seemed to leak out about his selflessness. He had picked up the torch of Bob Hope and spent every holiday with those serving in the armed forces overseas.

Brian sat on the stool in the ad with costumes from some of his most famous roles on hangers in the background. Changing images of characters that he'd played were projected around him.

Here is what he said.

"Hi, I'm Brian Edge. I'm an actor. That means I make a living playing dress up and make believe. I say words others have written in carefully crafted scripts. I get to speak phrases and ideas I couldn't begin to imagine myself — but I'm glad someone did.

Once upon a time I was in the service, the Army, and was the best potato peeler in my company. I happened to serve at a time where my assignment was the dangers and hazards of Ft. Gordon, Georgia. I got sunburned several times. I even spent a week in the hospital once with the flu.

"These days I get to pretend to be both famous and imaginary characters to do heroic, brave, and daring deeds — with the help of superb crews of stunt men and women. Sometimes I do stupid and funny things created to give you laughs.

"But I've never studied politics — nor ever openly supported any politician. You could say I've been in the closet politically.

"What I want to say to you now is — be careful from whom you take political advice. Thinking that actors, who have played great people, know themselves more than you — about *anything* — like political — is like consulting a tree surgeon about having your appendix removed. Kinda' dumb.

"I've seen and known some real heroes — men and women who have put their lives on the line so you could have the chance to vote. Some have paid with their lives and some with arms and legs, scars and burns you wouldn't believe unless you met them. But they did it for you.

"Don't squander that gift by not understanding what you're voting for or against. Take the time to really know what your vote means. And remember someone paid a very high price so you could vote. Don't waste it."

※

THE NOW THIRTY THREE YEAR-OLD CHIEF OF STAFF, GRAHAM Newcome, sat opposite Vice President Sundee Ives, 51, on couches in the Oval Office. The always pleasant VP was a contrast to the eternally serious Chief-of-Staff. Porter was in a padded chair between the two.

Also on the couch beside Graham was Cinnamon Higdon, Communications Director.

"Am I asking too much of you three to run things while I'm out running for office?" the President asked.

Vice President Ives' expression changed to a more sardonic smile as she said, "Not too much — but it has assured me that I never want the job. So take care of yourself."

"I'll do my best," Porter smiled back.

"Mrs. Ives and both your and her staffs here are very capable, Mr. President," Graham said. The recent unheralded birthday boy, remembered only by the President and Cinnamon, had to use all his efforts not to even casually glance at the lovely lady beside him.

"I must admit my hand's a little sore at the end of the day," the VP said. "And I thought I'd shaken a lot of hands before. But a photo op is a photo op."

"Some members of the staff wish they were out on the trail, Sir," Cinnamon said. "I think they understand the importance of keeping the home fires burning here."

"Good. I was sure I could count on all of you, but I'm also aware of the strain involved. And I'm sure there will be some major turnovers if Tracy and I pull this off. Have either of you noticed that the toll is too much on anyone?"

"No, Sir," the Chief-of-Staff answered.

"I've had my people help out and that, I think, has eased the pressure some," Vice President Ives said. "I've not picked up on any in-fighting. Have you, Graham?"

"I think I'm the last one they'd want to reveal that to," he said.

"What I have heard," Cinnamon chimed in, "is the people around here are all behind you — not just you and Mrs. Holyoak but also the amendments."

"How about leaks?"

"Surprisingly the loyal-to-the-core Democrats on my team," the VP said, "are feeling more loyalty to you, Mr. President, than even they expected. And I suspect they are on guard not to let others leak things."

"I concur," Chief-of-Staff Newcome said.

Cinnamon also agreed.

"Excellent," Porter said. "I'm about to embark on a week and a half tour. Tracy is going her own way and we'll meet up at the end for a joint rally. Are there any signs our foreign enemies are planning to take advantage of the campaign?"

The VP yielded to Graham.

"Sir, I don't think they have a grasp of how our way of governance works — especially campaigns and transitions of power. They try to meddle and cause discord but without any focused goal. I think they very much approve of a three way race but don't know which horse to back."

"Good to know."

THE LAST PERSON PORTER WANTED TO OFFICIALLY TOUCH BASE WITH before he left the White House was Cinnamon Higdon, his attractive and intelligent Director of White House Communications. The 5 foot 7 inch beauty of mixed heritage had been first in her class at Stanford Law School. Originally hired by President Leo Gibson, Cinnamon was only a lowly White House Communications staff member when her former boss died. It was Porter who discovered her talents and abilities when he assumed the Presidency. He promoted her to head the Communications shop after firing the woman who had held the job and who thought she ruled the White House. These days Cinnamon also filled in as Press Secretary because Grant Yarbrough, a former CNN News anchor, had stepped down to become a part of the Democratic Party's next election campaign. This was before Porter had decided to run for the office.

Cinnamon's coal dark hair always had the luster of a TV shampoo model. One of the aspects about this 35 year old source of power and insight was the fact that she seemed totally ignorant or at lease oblivious to her striking glamour.

"How are you holding up?" Porter asked her as she took the chair beside his desk.

"Never better, Mr. President. Why do you ask?"

"I'm aware of the weight you've assumed since Grant left."

"Does it show?" she joked looking down at the waist.

They both laughed.

It was Cinnamon's office who kept track of all of the President's correspondence — sending letters of congratulations, praise, and condolences whenever required. Porter had asked that such letters be sent to those making Eagle Scout or Golden Eaglet of Merit for the Girl Scouts — even though the two organizations had officially merged. It was also important to Porter that letters went out to Gold Star Parents of fallen soldiers and personal notes went to the wounded military members wherever in the world they might be. This alone was a considerable task.

Speeches were always in different stages of preparedness. Speeches, for example, for the death or incapacitation for major world leaders as well as members of Congress, the Supreme Court, and key functionaries throughout the administration were ready or near ready. Thus the amount of information readily on hand by this office was considerable and of a wide berth. The Communications people had to be aware of what was being said in all the major and even minor media formats as well as on Internet social sites.

The office also fielded questions from individual reporters and significant news sources. This, at times, required the drafting of position papers on matters which have heretofore not been on the President's radar.

Porter's request that the campaign and the White House staffs remain independent was a challenge for both teams. The campaign teams were constantly requesting information for ads and speeches they were preparing. Additionally the White House Office of Communications had to make quick decisions on what was possible to reveal and what was still in the nature of "classified" material and not for public consumption.

"I want you to know how much I appreciate your being here while I'm out playing politics."

"Hardly *playing*, Mr. President."

"That will depend on the outcome, I think."

"You know I'd like to be on the road with you, Sir — but it appears you have a solid team there."

"And I'd love to have you out there with us — but I consider the fate of the nation a much higher priority than any campaign. That's why you are so important to me to be here."

"One thing I've learned from you, Mr. President, is that service to the nation comes before anything personal."

"I appreciate that. And your efforts and devotion do not go unnoticed nor unappreciated."

"Anything you need, Mr. President. No questions asked."

"I am humbled and honored, Cinnamon. That's the message I want you to understand above and beyond anything else."

"Got it, Sir."

CHAPTER 13

Howard Sterling and Saundra's chapter on "Fake News and Other Nefarious Creations" turned out to be a more involved project than either of them expected.

During their research they were able to trace *fake news* all the way back to the 13th century B.C. It was here with Egyptian Pharaoh Rameses the Great. He was the most renowned and powerful leader of what was known as "the New Kingdom" of Egypt. He made himself the hero and winner of a war with the Hittites that in truth ended in a stalemate.

Another significant fake news story was created by the Roman ruler Octavian who succeeded his grandfather Julius Caesar after his assassination. He formed the Second Triumvirate with Mark Antony and Marcus Lepidus in order to defeat those who had murdered Caesar. Octavian took on the name of Augustus and managed to have Marcus Lepidus exiled. Then Augustus began a misinformation campaign against his remaining rival. Mark Antony was portrayed in stories, speeches, and songs as a drunkard, womanizer, and mere stooge of Cleopatra. A will, purported to be that of Mark Antony, declared that upon his death he wished to be buried with the Egyptian pharaohs. In the battle of Actium, a naval clash, known as The Final War of the Roman Republic, Antony and Cleopatra were defeated. Soon after, Mark Antony committed suicide because he believed a fake story Cleopatra had created that she was dead.

Christians were the victims of fake news during the 2nd and 3rd centuries. Stories were widely told of those who followed Christ. These fake tales said Christians also preached and practiced incest and cannibalism. Thousands were slaughtered because of these made up tales.

Jews became the causalities in the Austria-Hungarian city of Trent in 1475. The story this time was that a 2 and a half year-old Christian child had been murdered by members of the Jewish community. The end result was the torture and murder of 15 Jews who were burned at the stake.

Readers would, of course, be aware of the Salem, Massachusetts witchcraft trials of 1692 and '93. Over 200 people were accused and 19 tried and found guilty. Fourteen women and 5 men were hanged while one man, who refused to even plead, was crushed to death.

The hoax of the Cardiff Giant was a fake news story supported by a host of American newspapers in 1869. A New York atheist and tobacconist, named George Hull decided to create the giant statue. This came about following an argument at a Methodist revival about the existence of Nephilim, giants, in Genesis chapter 6 verse 4. The King James verse said there were giants who had lived on the earth.

Hull had a large slab of marble quarried for the supposed purpose of having a statue of Abe Lincoln made. Instead he had the block shipped to Chicago where he hired a German stonecutter, named Edward Burghardt, to carve the likeness of a giant man. The stonecutter was paid and sworn to secrecy.

Next Hull had the statue shipped to a cousin and buried on his farm land. A year later Hull hired men to dig an oil well where they discovered the statue. A tent was erected and by paying 50 cents each, wagonloads of people made the trek to Cardiff to see the unearthed giant.

Although scientists reported that the statue was a fake, the interest continued. The statue was shipped to Syracuse, New York, for a grander display. The object drew such crowds that Hull sold his interest in it for $48,000. Showman P.T. Barnum was willing to pay $50,000 for the statue but the new owners refused to sell. So Barnum had a wax and then plaster cast made of the statue from drawings and took it on the road. Barnum, who always claimed there was a sucker born every minute, touted his object as the real one and claimed the one in Syracuse to be a fake.

A year later Hull confessed the hoax to the press and both objects were declared to be fakes in a court of law. The owners of the original were then denied the right to sue Barnum for having claimed the statue in New York was a fake — because they both were.

What very few readers these days were aware of was the power of fake news for the so-called good of journalism. The much lauded Pulitzer Prize for Journalism was started by one of the biggest purveyors of fake news. The term *"yellow journalism," "tabloid journalism,"* and later *"checkbook journalism"* all evolved out of a type of newspaper which was first published on cheap paper that quickly yellowed.

The original standard purveyors of such journalism featured stories that bore no relationship to the truth in the stories they published. What followed was not really journalism. It was merely published information intentionally slanted to produce outrage, disgust, or shock. It was fellow yellow journalist, publisher William Randolph Hearst, using his widely read New York Journal, who helped goad the United States into the Spanish-American War. In 1897 Hearst received a cable from Cuba by his artist Frederic Remington, which read in part, "...there will be no war." Hearst responded with his own message — "You provide the pictures, and I'll provide the war." Following the explosion of the battleship USS Maine in the harbor of Havana, Cuba, the US did go to war.

President William McKinley tried to ignore the drum beats for war by the yellow press. The Democrats in Congress ultimately pushed him into a war he did not want. The fighting lasted only 10 weeks and the US won easily sinking two Spanish squadrons, one in Cuba and the other in Manila Bay of the Philippines.

RELUCTANT CANDIDATE

More recent examples of fake news all validate Communists founder Vladimir Lenin's observation that if you tell a lie often enough it becomes dogma, then a truth, and men will die for it. Joseph Goebbels, the head of Nazi propaganda, certainly believed in and practiced it to an art form. Even today there are those who do not and will not believe in the Jewish Holocaust because of lies Goebbels told and published during World War II.

Modern day fake news seems to date back to the cover-up of Edward Kennedy's abandoning Mary Jo Kopecne to drown in a car. This was in the summer of 1969 on Chappaquiddick Island.

Fake news next appeared in CBS anchor Dan Rather's false report about presidential candidate George Bush's service in the Air National Guard.

Other stories include Hillary Clinton's tale of being under enemy fire when visiting US troops — the anti-Muslim video tape which supposedly caused the attack on the US Embassy in Benghazi, Libya — the disproven claims against conservative Supreme Court Justice, Bret Kavanagh — the Black Lives Matter fiction of "Hands up - don't shoot" — to the fake crimes against liberals which were proven to be staged by the supposed victims, like the black TV star who staged an attack on himself.

Issues of omission as well as overt commission were also addressed in the chapter. Often what the media didn't cover or didn't shine a powerful enough spotlight on was more important than what it chose to cover. As several landmark studies had revealed, there was a consequential bias to the left by the majority of main stream media. The public trust in the past decade had gone from 3/4 in support of big media to a 75% mistrust. As Howard and Saundra pointed out, this was in large part a self-inflicted sucking chest wound of the media's own laps in standards and practices.

The most often sighted example of this was outside politics. It was the rush to coverage of all issues Islamic and an almost total denial/abandonment of Christian issues. The murder of the 19 Muslims in a New Zealand mosque by a white supremacist in 2019 was a prime example. Yet, headlined news and news segments focused on this tragedy alone. Standard media meanwhile ignored the slaughter of

120 Nigerian Christians by 50 Fulani Muslim militants at the same time.

Howard and Saundra called attention to the old tale that the word "news" comes from sign posts which point to North, East, West, and South — N.E.W.S. The point of news was to keep people informed of events happening all over their world. Instead it had come down to the ol' saying, "news is what the editor says is news." It also put to shame the slogan of The Gray Lady, The New York Times, hypothetically our nation's "paper of record." Across the banner top of the front page is the motto, "All the news that's fit to print."

It was 1897 when then owner, Adolph S. Ochs, created the famous slogan. It was his declaration of the papers impartially. But like that age, the sentiment had lost its luster just as the profession of journalism had tarnished itself by both ill-conceived words, lack of judicious and ethical standards of fairness and balance.

However, the biggest fake news story of all was the Trump/Russia Conclusion hoax. Leading the charge was The New York Times, The Washington Post, CNN, MSNBC and INK. The hole created in public trust of media was so large and damaging that the distrust cast its shadow and doubt for years. The loss of trust in such institutions as the FBI, the CIA, and the US Justice Department could never be healed.

The bottom line was that a crime of collusion between the sitting US President and the state of Russia, was never discovered or proven by any investigating unit — from the FBI to assorted Congressional committees. It was just a politically driven conspiracy by the Democrats, who refused to accept the fact that their candidate, Hillary Clinton, lost a race that was considered a done deal from the very beginning. That is what brought shame and deep seated doubt on all of those who kept assuring the public that what they hoped for was really true.

As in all fake news, present and past, facts didn't and don't matter. It is and always was the basic belief of the story that drives its narrative and warped perceptions — even after the facts come out and the truth is known.

Thus journalism had cut its own throat, shot itself in the foot, and cried wolf too often to be believed at first glance ever again. It was a self-imposed curse fed by colleges and university journalism programs which had totally lost their way and had come to believe the opinions were as good as the facts. The public simply had quit buying it.

CHAPTER 14

The Democrats had taken the campaign tact that Porter Randall had lied to the public when only days into his assumed office he had said he had no ambitions to seek the presidency.

"It sounds to me like he was against it before he was for it," Senator George Tossen said as if it were off the cuff. He was sitting in the backseat of an open convertible talking to the media as he approached a rally site. The intent was the possibility of making Tossen look as much like FDR, our nation's longest serving president, as shown in old pictures. Of course, the remark had been carefully scripted and even rehearsed before it seemed to fall effortless from the candidate's lips.

What the Democrats were trying to avoid by making this charge was the comparison between Tossen himself and former Democratic Senator and Secretary of State John Kerry. In 2002 Kerry famously voted in favor of the US war with Iraq. Months later he became a powerful anti-war voice claiming to have been against that same war. Although not his exact words, the controversy became known by the phrase, "He was for it before he was against it." The expression became a tag the Massachusetts Senator found himself stamped with as he flip flopped on issues in the rest of his career.

The Republicans took the angle that only by the strictest legal definition was Randall allowed to be sworn into the vacant office of the President. It was the best wording House Speaker Vincent Sturges had managed to come up with. It was an attempt to cover his unbridled anger and bitterness for having missed out on the chance to be President himself. Still, technically, he was not holding the office of House Speaker at the time of Leo Gibson's sudden death. This was the fact Sturges could never accept.

The problems with both attacks were that they were *against* something and not *for* anything. It was the conservative media voices who pointed this out — an obvious observation no one in the liberal/progressive media were willing to mount. If they pointed it out even against the Republicans, it would reveal the Democrats clear choice of having taken the same route.

VP candidate Tracey Holyoak made her swing to the far West of the nation while Porter took on the East Coast. It was quickly becoming clear that both candidates were drawing larger and larger crowds. Mrs. Holyoak proved herself to be a more inspiring speaker than anyone expected. Both the Democrats and the Republicans had to change tactics and quickly.

In a secret meeting at the Four Season's Lionshead Resort in Vail, Colorado, strategists from both traditional camps met in their first joint effort to combat the growing Randall/Holyoak threat.

The working group's first idea was to attack the proposed amendments which both established parties opposed with equal fervor. First, TV and social media ads would claim that both ideas to alter the Constitution were being properly handled by the prescribed legislative process. It was maintained that the legislative way was what the founders of the nation intended. In effect the commercials were saying, "If it ain't broke, don't fix it."

This assertion came to earth in a crash when Tracy Holyoak began pointing out that the 26th amendment, the one granting the right to vote for 18 year-olds, took only 3 months and 8 days to be ratified through the Congressional process. The proposed 28th and 29th amendments have both been stuck in Congressional committees for a year and a half — and no one believed they were ever to make it to the floor of Congress for a vote.

Neither the Democrats nor the Republicans could fight this logic and their ads and that approach were soon dropped.

As usual the Democrats wanted to offer more and more free programs without offering any methods of paying for them. They added free trade school training to their free college proposal. The price tag for this and their other give-a-ways was never even mentioned nor were their impact on the national debt. But at least they were proving to be in favor of something.

The Republicans turned to their old themes of smaller government and lower taxes but without specifics. Few in Congress wanted to see any government program operating in their state or district to fall under the ax. In order to trim government spending, this would be precisely what would have to happen.

When Porter took to the podium at his rally in Pennsylvania, he paraphrased John Adams. "Fear is the foundation of most governments in history. But it is so sordid and brutal a reason for being — that it is what makes America different in all of the world. Those who want a bigger and more intrusive government are asking for misery and oppression."

"Remember the lyrics," Porter said next, "to Jonathan Edwards song 'Sunshine, Sunshine'? The words, 'He can't run his own life — I'll be damn if he'll run mine.'

"What part of government do you think can run your life better than you can? What has been the result of government intrusion of health care? Do you still have your own doctor? Do you still have your own insurance? Has it cost you less?

"What has government ever done so well you are willing to say, 'Here, you take over my life and tell me what to do — and I'll do just what you say?'

"Ronald Reagan said, 'We are a nation that has a government — not the other way around. And that makes us special among the nations of the earth.' What we need isn't more government — it's less. What we don't need is anything free from the government — because it's never free. Somebody has to pay for it — and eventually that somebody is you.

"We used to be a nation of doers and builders. We stood on our own two feet and asked for nothing but a fair chance — a level playing field — and we would and *could* compete with anyone. We have better ideas — better hearts — more love and forgiveness than any people in this world. We are as God has made us — free — independent — resourceful — resilient — powerful — loving — and kind. No nation in history has accomplished what we Americans have. And we did it together — as Americans. Not divided as others would have us — not as African/Americans, not as Hispanic/Americans, nor as Irish/Americans, nor as Jewish/Americans and not black or white or tan or red or anything — but as Americans — united."

The networks, cable channels and social media outlets hated to have to play Porter's quotes. His words and his infectious spirit came through. They liked to have reporters read his quotes without Porter's energy — but still his words in his own voice got out.

THE BIGGEST SURPRISE OF THE CAMPAIGN TURNED OUT TO BE AMELIA Morris, George Tossen's VP running mate. The *"new, bright shiny, thing"* from Massachusetts had been a media darling from her first day on the national stage. The blonde haired, green eyed woman was loved by the camera. She didn't appear to ever take a bad picture.

An obscure website had first chronicled the story of how the unmarried Ms. Morris had risen to power. Her previous position was senior manager of a national chain of coffee shops. She was a barista with over 10 years of experience. A group calling itself Liberty Through Honest Government had held a series of auditions for an unannounced project. The auditions were just like those for any play or a movie. Applicants would come on stage and either read, or, if they were fast learners, speak the words of the page to the audience of a half dozen. Through the narrowing process Amelia Morris became the winner.

She met all the requirements. She was a college graduate, holding a liberal arts degree from Lasell College in Auburndale, Massachusetts. She was a mediocre student but she hadn't failed any of her classes. A lifelong Massachusetts resident with enough smarts to be able to carry on an intelligent conversation, her major asset was her looks. Twice married and divorced, she was undeniably attractive. It was only after winning the audition that she learned the role was to play the part of a Member of the US Congress as a representative from her home state.

Knowing little to nothing about politics but able to be easily led by her "team" from Liberty Through Honest Government, she soon proved herself to be a more than adequate public speaker. In a district were the long serving Democrat had died after the revelation of a hidden gay sex life, Morris quickly became the favorite in the primary. In spite of significant Democratic Party money being poured in for other Democratic candidates, Amelia won the slot.

Speaking the words supplied by her handlers, Amelia Morris quickly gained media prominence — sometimes for her outrageous remarks against party leadership, but at times for her seemingly very progressive ideas with clever titles. By the middle of her first term she had become the unspoken leader to the far left side of the party and the absolute beloved of younger voters who watched her blogs and TV appearances with glee. She had a quick wit and could deliver a punch line like a professional.

Claims that she had been a sometimes-call-girl were never proven and more than a few of her accusers quit giving press interviews or died under mysterious circumstances.

At 35, Amelia met the requirements to be on the Democratic presidential ticket but only after she agreed to toe the established party line. This promise only lasted a little over a month before her off-handed remarks began going off the rails.

She was soon described by Democratic Party insiders as a loose cannon rolling across a ship's deck in rough seas while firing indiscriminately at both friend and foe. Still she had the undying support of the parties ultra-progressives. She supported free basic income even for those who did not choose to work as well as fully funded family vacations twice a year at corporation or government expense.

According to Amelia Morris, everything should be "single payer."

What she never said was that the single payer was the government and ultimately the taxpayer.

The Republicans loved her because of the damage she was doing to her own party. So did the media. Some reporters were constantly bombarding her with trick questions like, "As an island nation, should Brazil get full membership with the other landlocked nations of the European Union?" This one she had taken and responded that "Brazil should be equal to the rest of the E.U. Being an island nation should not detract from its place among the nations of Europe."

She tried to cover her gaff at her very next stop by saying she hadn't studied geography since high school and she wasn't very good at it then. But she did know what a *Brazilian* was. This didn't get the laughter she had hoped for and her handlers told her emphatically to not answer questions she didn't know the answer to — especially if the answers weren't in the scripts they had given her.

But it was the late night TV comics who had the last laugh. For several nights running Morris was the prime target for jokes. The most memorable of the lot was one that said, "A quick note to those of you who are close shavers. If you get a Brazilian, don't let them give you a Morris Brazilian — evidently they take part of your brain."

CHAPTER 15

Presidential Secretary, Gwendolyn Jacobs, was waiting for Porter when he boarded Air Force One to the next hop to Hartford, Connecticut. The 52 year-old usually was at her post, the desk just outside the door to the Oval Office. But wherever the President went, Gwendolyn went. She had a well trained staff to handle the incoming phone calls and endless Executive Branch paperwork at the White House. The President preferred to have Ms. Jacobs on the big plane with him whenever he traveled officially.

"Mr. President," she said as Porter removed his jacket and hung it on a hanger behind his desk in the airborne office. "Grant Yarbrough has been trying to catch you in an '*open moment*' for about a week. He calls at odd times but is never insistent. He understands your schedule and the demands on your time. But he called again about 15 minutes ago and I told him you were wrapping up a campaign stop. He said he was watching it on TV and that's why he called. He knows where I am and asked if he could hold on-line until you were back onboard."

"I thought Grant was working on the Tossen team," Porter said. He remembered the last conversation he had with the former CNN News Anchor who had become the Press Secretary for Leo Gibson and had stayed on when Porter ask if he could continue to do the job with no hidden agenda. Grant said he could and Porter hired him on the spot. But as the campaign season was warming up at the beginning of spring, Grant said he felt it was time for him to get back to Democratic politics. He expected to be involved with whichever candidates the party picked.

"He doesn't sound like that's what he doing, Mr. President — although he's not really said what he's up to or what he wants."

"I'll be glad to talk to him for a couple of minutes," Porter said.

"I'll connect you, Gwendolyn said closing the door to the President's office and returning to her station of a desk, computer, and telephone just behind the President's cabin.

Porter picked up the phone when the light flashed on his desk phone.

"Mr. Yarbrough, you are connected to President Randall," Gwendolyn said before hanging up herself.

"Mr. President," Grant began, "I will be brief."

"OK, Grant, but it's still good to hear from you. How's your side of the opposition doing?"

"That's the thing, Mr. President. I'm not on team Democrat. In fact, I've '*walked way*.'"

"Really," Porter was surprised. The handsome former cable newscaster would be a substantial asset to the Democrats, he thought.

"This is no longer the party I knew — nor the one my family had been a part of for as far back as I've been able to trace my roots." Grant's father had been a black Air Force sergeant, who had fallen in love with and married a Vietnamese beauty when he was stationed at the US Consulate in Hanoi after the war. "The rest of the story, "Grant said, "is that I'm very much between jobs. I don't want to take any of the network consultant ships I've been offered — I'd like to come back to work for you, Mr. President, if I'm still welcome."

"Grant, you were always an excellent Press Secretary. Is that what you're interested in?"

"No, Sir. I thought I might be of more use to your campaign team. I realize it would be a big story for me to come back to work for you — and I'm not afraid or ashamed to deal with that. The truth is, you have changed my way of thinking. In some ways I feel more like I did

89

in grade school when I thought ours was the greatest country in the world and we set the standard to doing what was right. I don't think either of the established parties represents that anymore."

"You know that no third party candidate has *ever* won the Presidency?" Porter asked.

"Very aware, Sir. But I'd still like to be a part of the one that does."

"If we do."

"I'm sure *we* will, Mr. President."

Porter thought for a moment and then said, "Grant, here's what I'll do. You know my campaign is being run by Ward Adair and Ella Suzuki."

"Yes, Sir. I know them both."

"Well, I'll hand you off to Ella, who is traveling with me now, and let her and Ward decide."

"That's very fair, Mr. President. They will probably be a great deal more suspicious of me than you are. But that's the way it should be."

"Then hold on, Grant." Porter put that call on hold and punched the button which connected him back to Gwendolyn Jacobs. When she was on the line, he said, "Gwen, could you switch this call to Ella Suzuki? She's somewhere on board."

"She standing right here, Mr. President. Let me give her time to get to her seat and I'll connect them."

"Thank you," Porter said.

On the second day of this campaign trip, Porter spotted Grant and Ella swapping papers at the back of the packed Greensburg, N.C., Coliseum Complex. Grant was quickly going off with his head in his cell phone.

When he had a chance to speak to Ella on the hop to Chattanooga, she said, "He's doing very well. Nothing is too menial and he's always ready to do more. He seems to be a real convert — but Ward still wants to keep him on a short leash for a while."

"I hope it works out," Porter said. "I thought he was an excellent Press Secretary."

"But he would also be an excellent plant from the Democrats. He knows we suspect that and appears to be playing everything straight."

RELUCTANT CANDIDATE

AIR FORCE ONE WAS IN THE AIR HEADED FOR COLUMBIA, SOUTH Carolina, when the President was interrupted grabbing a sandwich lunch with the First Lady, Deidra. Porter picked up the phone and Gwendolyn Jacobs said, "Mr. President, you have an urgent call from Mr. Chesterfield."

Porter punched the flashing button and said, "Victor?" Victor Chesterfield, Porter's first Chief-of-Staff was now Defense Secretary.

"Mr. President, there's been a terrorist attack on the VA hospital in Amarillo. Early reports make it sound like an Oklahoma City, Murrah Federal Building, type of bombing. No official death toll, but it's expected to be nearly as high as the '95 bombing."

In 1995 168 people, men, women, and children, had died when American Timothy McVeigh and co-conspirator Terry Nichols set off a powerful bomb in front of a US government building. McVeigh, a native of western New York, and Nichols were survivalists. McVeigh had served in the Persian Gulf War and was decorated with several medals for his service. But both men claimed the Murrah Building attack was payback. They were striking as revenge for two events. First was the August '92 shoot-out between federal agents and survivalist Randy Weaver at his rural cabin at Ruby Ridge, Idaho. Weaver's wife and a US Marshal were killed in the shootout. Secondly was the siege of April, '93 of a Branch Davidian religious sect near Waco, Texas. This fight claimed 75 cult members.

The early death count, according to Victor, was under 100. Porter said he was going to divert his flight to Amarillo and for Victor to let him know any and all news.

Porter connected with the Air Force One pilot and told him of the immediate flight change. The President took to the 761's passenger intercom to announce what he knew and why the plane was altering course. Within a minute, Deidra was in his office with him. She phoned Porter's sister, Irene Meehan, who was still living in one of the apartments in Blair House. Irene had served as First Lady when Porter had first assumed the Presidency since he was a widower at the time. Irene had taken on the VA as her cause of choice while she served. She then had shared the duty with Deidra who picked up the cause when she and Porter married. Irene and her husband, a retired NASA rocket scientist, who had become a personal advisor to Porter, were both on a charter flight to Amarillo within three hours.

Part of the problem of a traveling President is all the teams which must travel with him or be ahead of him as part of what is known as a lift package. A Marine air squadron with the President's Osprey, plus two more identical craft, moved the President and his entourage from Air Force One to other sites when ground travel wasn't the best option. The Secret Service detail which traveled with The Beast, the Presidential armored limo and three other limos, had its own C-5B Galaxy transport. All of these crafts had to be notified of the change in plans.

They landed at Amarillo's Rick Husband Airport. Bell Helicopter physically shared some of the same landing strips. Since the V-280 Valor, a twin engine rotor successor to the Osprey was being built there, one was available to the President. It was decided that the President would use this craft instead of waiting for his official shorter range planes to arrive.

CHAPTER 16

The Thomas E. Creek VA Medical Center was located at 6010 Amarillo Blvd West, a 4 lane East/West corridor across town. The facility was located on the top of a rise in what had become part of the cities medical district. The VA Center served the Texas Panhandle north of Lubbock as well as Oklahoma, Kansas and Eastern New Mexico.

Approaching by air, it was clear that the blast had demolished half of the main building. Additionally parts of the Emergency Services building to the left and the museum and other offices to the right were destroyed. There were few of the 17 buildings on site which didn't appear undamaged either by the explosion or resulting fires.

Three batteries of surface-to-air missiles formed a wide triangle across the space as well as sandbag-mounted machine gun emplacements. Snipers were perched atop mobile police mall security towers which had been moved in. Overhead two Air National Guard helicopter gunships and a Warthog, close- support fighter, circled.

The flashing lights of emergency vehicles of every description covered the campus, but a landing spot had been cleared for the President's V-280. The early August heat combined with that generated by the blazes were like a furnace when the President and First Lady stepped down. The fire, police, and uniformed military coordinators who met with Porter and Deidra either wore radio microphones on their uniforms or carried handheld devices. These were to enable them to give commands, relay information, or to stay informed as needed.

White House Photographer, Leigh Janda, moved around getting snapshots of both the damage and the actions of the President and First Lady.

Fifty-four year-old Air Force Brigadier General Terry Becker, flat top hair and piercing gray eyes, was the military officer in charge. He had been on an inspection tour of aircraft in development at Bell Helicopter when word of the bombing reached him. He flew to the site and assumed command getting in touch with the Pentagon to report what the on-the-ground situation was. It was Becker who briefed Porter and Deidra.

"They took out most of the main reception building and part of the ER there on the left, Mr. President."

"Why all the extra heavy security?" Porter yelled to be heard over the spinning props of the V-280.

"There's no strategic significance to the hospital, Sir, but one of our working theories is that the purpose was to draw you out."

"So you're telling me I'm putting more people in danger just by being here?"

"Possible, Mr. President. But — personally I'm glad you came. So is everyone here."

"Then, General, let me do what good I can. Take me to the survivors. And I want to speak to the first responders before I leave."

"Yes, Sir," the General said holding onto his hat and leading the group away from the prop wash of the plane.

"Have we met before, General?" Porter asked as they moved.

"No, Sir — but you did commandeer my ride the night President Gibson died and you needed to get from Amarillo to DC in a hurry."

"That was kind of rude of me," Porter said.

"Not at all, Sir. I work for you."

"Yes, but still —."

"You did send me a letter of apology later that week, Mr. President. And I'm ashamed to say I've been kind of an ass about it."

"How so?"

"I framed the letter and have it hanging on my office wall."

Porter grinned. "I don't see anything wrong with that. But if I do get killed here today, you'll have to take that letter down."

"Yes, Sir. I'm very well aware of that."

As soon as the group escorted the President and First Lady out of the immediate roar of the plane's engine, Porter asked, "What's the causality count at the moment?"

"Seventy-seven, Sir. We expect close to 100 by the time it's all said and done."

"What do we know about how it was pulled off?"

"Of course all the security cameras were blown to hell, but their storage units were in another building — so we have everything up to the moment of the blast. They used a 25 passenger handicap bus — obviously packed to the ceiling with explosives — military grade explosives."

"Where'd the bus come from?"

"Buses of this kind have been stolen here and there around the area for the past couple of months. Usually they're found abandoned with a little vandalism in 2 to 3 days. It was thought to be kids — even a gang at work. Now we believe it was all practice for the real thing."

"Suicide bombing?"

"That's one of the strange parts. From the footage we can see the bus door open and a man in kakis starting to get out just as it blows. We can't see any triggering device in his hands. We're thinking it was remotely detonated. The driver may have thought he was going to just drive the bus, park it and walk away. It didn't work out that way."

Over the next hour Porter and Deidra visited with the wounded who were in hastily converted facilities on the site. Beds were in the halls and packed with 5 to 6 patients in each available room. Nurses and doctors in blood soaked scrubs worked quickly on each patient before moving onto their next victim. It was clear these people had combat military field hospital experience from the way they worked.

The pictures Leigh Janda captured would become the best living record of the events. There were the heroics of the medical professionals and the stoicism of the victims, many of whom refused treatment telling the doctors and nurses to help people who really needed their efforts.

The President and First Lady prayed with some victims, and one picture showed them stepping out of one room of casualties just as an orderly was pulling the bloody sheet over the face of one woman who didn't make it.

After a little over an hour and 20 minutes, after speaking to several first responders, Porter and Deidra were back in the air as all those trying to work the scene had suggested. On his way back to DC.

By then a heretofore unknown ISIS group in Africa was claiming credit for the attack and pledged there were others about to happen.

Porter broadcast a live-feed to all the networks praising the work of everyone involved in the Amarillo VA endeavor.

For the first time in history, a sitting US President spoke to the nation from aboard Air Force One. He spoke at 5 PM Eastern Standard Time, 4 Central, and 3 Mountain Standard Time, and 2 Pacific.

Invoking the Presidential authority under the 14th Amendment, Porter called both houses of Congress into session beginning in 2 days. Congress was officially on its August recess to campaign. It was a traditional political season for those up for reelection in either house or for the candidate of their party for President.

The first time this Presidential power was used was in March, 1797, when President John Adams called on Congress to suspend relations with France. The action had been taken 26 times before, lastly by President Harry Truman who called Congress back also during their August recess.

This time Porter set the agenda by naming the key items of the immigration mess. First was the process by which a person became citizen — meaning the elimination of the "birth right" clause as a path to citizenship — border security, including manpower and facility needs for both the US Border Patrol and the Immigration, Customs and Enforcement agencies — sanctuary cities — immigration detention and deporting — elimination of immigrant welfare in any form — e-verify for immigrant workers — and assimilation requirements, meaning the learning of English and subscribing to US laws and customs over all others.

"This is a national emergency," Porter said. "I will sign a declaration to that effect within an hour of reaching the White House. We have declared war on no one but war has been declared on us. We must respond in a fashion equal to that state of being.

"I will campaign no more this next two weeks and you should demand that your Representatives and Senators do the same. Let's attend to the nation's business in Washington immediately. There is work for our country which must be done."

CHAPTER 17

There were three days of funerals in Amarillo for the total of 93 victims from the VA hospital bombing. Both the Democrats and the Republicans, as well as the media, tried to make hay of the fact that Porter and Deidra left DC while Congress was still in Special Session. However, besides the Amarillo funerals, the First Couple also attended two funerals the next week at Arlington National Cemetery after they returned to DC.

Some media outlets claimed the President and First Lady had returned to Texas for a vacation. They and the few politicians who went on camera to make the same claim were blasted on social media for their comments. This came especially when images, sometimes in the same newscast, showed the First Couple at the funerals.

Within less than a week the FBI had rounded up 11 members of the terrorist cell responsible for the Amarillo attack. They were all Islamic radicals and a **surprising** number of the group were women. Surveillance video revealed members casing the hospital weeks before the attack, and a lucky break came with the footage of their stealing the passenger van.

The abandoned workshop were the explosives were gathered, prepared and loaded on the bus was also discovered. Other leads were kept under wraps as the FBI, the CIA, and the military followed the threads all over the world.

PORTER CALLED A MEETING THE DAY THE NEW IMMIGRATION BILL was sent to him after passing both Houses of Congress. Vice President Sundee Ives was the first to arrive. A moment later pock-marked faced Chief-of-Staff, Graham Newcome, held the door open for White House Comms Director, Cinnamon Higdon. No one noticed the tiny smile Graham wore as Cinnamon passed him.

Now they were all in attendance. Porter reintroduced Ward Adair and Ella Suzuki to everyone.

"You all know I wanted to keep the running of the Administration separated as much as possible from the campaign. We've just pasted a point where that is no longer possible. I believed the most positive thing that came out of the Amarillo attack would be this new law," Porter lifted the leather bound folders set for Presidential signature. He dropped it on his desk with a bang.

The pressure on Congress from the electorate had forced the immigration issue. The resulting legislation had addressed the key points Porter had outlined in his agenda when calling the special session.

"Congress knows that their new law is unconstitutional," Porter said, "but I have to sign it.

"It blatantly violates the Constitution," Graham said.

"Any first year law student who stayed half-awake could file a legitimate suit to freeze it and have it declared unconstitutional," Ward Adair said leaning forward from his position on one of the couches.

"This law was a stop gap measure and we all know it," Graham agreed. "It's supposed to appease you, Mr. President, and anyone clamoring for an immigration fix."

"It will be challenged in Federal Court before your signature is even dry," Cinnamon added. "And rightly so. This is a sham law."

"But Congress has acted," Porter said. "and they've done everything I asked for.

"Yes," Ella Suzuki said with a sly grin, "but these words are not yours — they're from Congress. They have put in writing exactly what is needed — even if they did it knowing it would never be enforced."

"So what," Ward said to his wife, "are you proposing a third Constitutional Amendment for the campaign?"

"No. There's still one more way to go about this."

THE LEADERS OF BOTH PARTIES PUT OUT THE WORD THAT SINCE Congress had acceded to the President's demands, it was only fair that he sign the bill on live TV.

This was a mid-afternoon event with the President sitting at his desk and Congressional leaders crowded around him on both sides. When the red light of the camera came on, Porter began to speak.

"In chapter three of the book of Ecclesiastes it says, 'To everything there is a season, and a time to every purpose under heaven. A time to be born, and a time to die; a time to plant, and a time to pluck up that which is planted...' and it also says, there is a '...time to build up and a time to break down.'

"Today is a time to break down. The bill before me — the Tossen/Sturges Immigration Act was written to address each of the requests I made following the horrible attack on the VA hospital in Amarillo. It was carefully worded, and carefully considered. It proved how quickly Congress can act when it wants to."

Behind the President the Congressional party was beaming.

"It was, however, never designed to be enforceable law. It is unconstitutional to its very core. I am therefore vetoing this measure — "Porter scrawled "VETO" across the page and signed it at the bottom.

The looks of confusion and shock were plain to see on the faces of those around the President.

"Instead I am calling for a measure on the ballot of every state and territory giving citizens the chance to vote to decide if theirs will be one of the necessary 34 states required to pass a resolution calling for A Convention of States — according to Article 5 of our Constitution. The exact wording of Article 5 is now posted on the White House website. Come this November, let the American citizens decide if this nation, as Lincoln so eloquently put it, '...that this nation, under God, shall have a new birth of freedom — and that government of the people, by the people, for the people, shall not perish from the earth.'

"Good day — and may God bless these United States of America."

※

THOSE ATTENDING WHAT THEY THOUGHT WAS GOING TO BE A signing ceremony, which would ultimately come back to bite the unelected President in the ass, were humiliated beyond words. Most stormed out of the Oval office as the red light on the video camera blinked out.

Pundits on every channel were caught totally unprepared for what they had just witnessed. While there were thousands of words ready on paper and teleprompter to laugh at the stupidity of the President — and even a few to praise him — for a symbolic victory of the signed bill, none were ready to deal with the call for a Convention of States.

Some immediately turned to their constitutional scholars on set ready to rip the President's action apart. However even these few experts were not ready with refined, cultured or in-depth comments about the President's action.

A Convention of States for the propose of amending the Constitution, was laid out in Article 5 of the original draft of the Constitution. It required two-thirds, currently 34, of the legislatures of the states, or an act of Congress, to call for such a convention. If it came by way of Congress, two-thirds of both houses must agree. Of the current 27 amendments, all had come through acts of Congress.

Calls for a Convention of States for a balanced budget had been issued before but never achieved the needed threshold of state support.

The previous calls for an "Article V Convention" based on a single issue — balanced budget and even Congressional Behavior — didn't materialize. The lack of action on the items never fully died — but neither were they fully realized.

It was unclear whether such a convention, an Article 5 convention, or Convention of States — once summoned would or could be legally bound to limits of its original call. That's the fear. Once such a convention got approved, there was no way to stop it. It could totally rewrite the Constitution or alter any of its provisions, large or small.

It was Porter's position that it was better to trust the citizens than professional politicians. The danger of an uninformed electorate was always a threat. The media, having become so biased, knew that it was impossible to know what the end result might be. Congress had, in effect, forced Porter's hand and the new battle for the soul of America was on.

CHAPTER 18

All the campaigns began again the day after the televised veto. The "War On Congress" became the battle cry of both the Democrats and the Republicans.

Porter's people arranged for his first day back to be a media blitz. He appeared on TV morning shows, mid-day talk shows, and in between different national radio call-in shows. The cap of the day was the President's appearance on the long-running TV talk show, "Liberty, Justice and Onassis."

The schedule was arranged so that Porter had time for a nap and what the Secret Service refered to as "...discussions of the Austro-Hungarian issue..." with the First Lady. This was code for very personal time together for the First Couple. It was true that there was both aggression and submission involved in such *"discussions"* as well as a final negotiated peace settlement — although if it ever appeared in writing the word "peace" would be spelled "piece."

In the studio that evening a very rested and rejuvenated Porter Randall sat in a comfortable chair across from a man with thick white hair who had been called the "master of DC politics" and "the Greek God of intelligent conversation."

Alexander Barnabas Onassis had a daily one hour TV show of his own where he discussed the issues of the day and his insights into them. "A.B." as Onassis was called by his close friends, was a native of the mid-west and an Oxford Rhodes scholar. He had also served in the Marines as a platoon leader in Afghanistan. Decorated for heroism, he never talked about his medals nor his time in the Pentagon and the Department of Justice where he learned the truth of life *"inside the beltway"* — as existence in and around DC were known. He was no relation to the famous Greek shipping magnet who had married opera singer Maria Callas and later Jackie Kennedy, the widow of J.F.K. He said even his DNA proved it. Even if he were kin, Onassis said, his side of the family would be the land-locked, dry side of the family.

The set for the show looked like the library of a prestigious university. There were portraits of the American founding fathers back-lit on the wall among the shelves of leather bound books. A large world globe was in the background as well as an early astronomer's telescope. The two men sat at what could have been a round library study table with coffee and books stacked among papers.

After the President's introduction, Onassis went to his very first question.

"You are in a job you never wanted nor aspired to."

"Correct," was Porter's single word answer.

"And yet you are now campaigning for that very office. How can you balance those two ideas?"

"I hoped I never would have to. The reason I'm in this race is not so much to get elected to the Presidency as it is to see that the two amendments I have supported from the very beginning get their needed attention before the public."

"We'll go into that in depth in a few minutes. First can you tell us something about Porter Randall we don't know?"

"I like French dip sandwiches."

"I was thinking more in terms of your background."

Onassis had a dark colored clipboard in his lap with pale yellow paper and a series of typed questions and notes. Some critics said it reminded them of the famous conservative author, columnist, and TV host, William F. Buckley.

"You started out as a surgeon, didn't you, Mr. President? An Army surgeon. Is that right?"

"Well, if the truth be told, I believe I started out years before that."

"As what?"

"An average student of lower middle class parents. I wasn't much interested in school until I got to junior high — as we used to call it the — what is now middle school. There I really discovered science. I was born and grew up in Texas — in a town called Corsicana — a good 50 miles Southeast of Dallas."

"The town's known for its fruitcakes I believe."

"That and mattresses. The town was established in 1848 by Jose Antonio Navarro and named after the Mediterrian Island of Corsica where his father was born."

"Navarro was a Mexican and a Texas revolutionary hero wasn't he?"

"He was — but he quickly began thinking of himself as a Texan. Not a Mexican/Texan. He was a good friend of Stephen F. Austin and the two men shared the same vision for Texas."

"And your early vision?"

"I just wanted to be a doctor — a physician. It wasn't until I got into the Unified Services Military Medical School that my interest turned to surgery."

"Why did you decide on that medical school?"

"Primarily because neither my family nor I could afford any other medical. You go to the SMMS and you come out an officer with an 8 year commitment to the military. I was fine with that. Some of the best hospitals in the world and the newest and best equipment are in the service."

"You had more than a few jobs growing up, didn't you?"

"Paperboy, life guard, welder's helper, roofer's assistant, auto parts delivery driver — I don't even remember all of them."

"And you became a surgeon in a M*A*S*H hospital in Afghanistan?"

"The last military front line hospital to be called a M*A*S*H was the 212th in Iraq. That was back in 2003, I believe. Today they're called Combat Support Hospitals. Larger, faster, helicopters have made transport time shorter. Bigger facilities can handle more equipment and staff."

"Then after your service you and a partner ran a day surgical clinic in Amarillo."

"We did."

"Why did you choose Amarillo?"

"It was an underserved area of what they call West Texas. To most people who live there, it's the Texas Panhandle."

"So you saw a need and you went to fill it."

"You could say that, yes."

"But you stopped your surgical practice after your first wife was killed in a tragic plane crash."

"That was the most difficult thing I've ever had to face. For a couple of years I wasn't much good to anyone — not even myself."

"But you didn't become an alcoholic or a drug abuser?"

"No drugs because I had seen too many of the bad effects both in the service and out from the wrong use of drugs. And I really can't take any credit for not becoming an alcoholic — I simply couldn't stand the taste of booze. I had a friend who stayed close to me during those years who told me it was because I had probably been a drunk in a previous life. I don't know about that, but alcohol was never a choice for me."

"How did you get into Congress?"

"I had started writing fiction — had a couple of moderate successes with them, but it wasn't like I had a day job. Some friends convinced me to run for an open seat in the House. My platform was to try and find a way to funnel the water that collects in playa lakes."

"Playa lakes?"

"That's a Spanish term for what many people would call a dry lake. It's a place where water collects in the wet seasons or during storms. They're all over the mid-west ranching and farming fields."

"So, you wanted to collect and funnel this water. Where did you intend for it to go?"

"Into the aquifers — the massive underground lakes that feed our farms and ranch lands."

"How were you going to accomplish this?"

"Our plan was to develop some technology which would make it possible for a farmer or rancher — or even a city or town — to have a simple pump of some sort that would go in the middle of the lake and return the water down to replenish the aquifers. It usually takes several hundred years for ground water to seep down and filter through the rocks and gravel to refill an aquifer. We thought that — a way could be found to speed up the process. Most of these playa lakes just sit there and eventually dry up until the next storm or two refill them. Some even cause flooding during the next small rainstorm. Usually any crop planted there will be drowned — or withered. The ground in Oklahoma is mostly for grazing except for when its playa lakes are full — or have become mud bogs. Then it kills cattle or anything else that gets stuck in it."

"All right, you were a member of the House of Representatives. A Democrat or a Republican?"

"Independent. I usually met with or caucused with the Republicans."

"And how did that get you into the White House?"

"It was Christmas during my second term. It was right after the big Internet Scandal. Remember that?"

"Oh, yes."

"Well, the Speaker of the House at the time, Budd Elliot, was one of those caught up in the scandal. He resigned. The House was left without a Speaker."

"Wouldn't the majority Whip assume the office?"

"Not according to House rules. A new Speaker had to be elected. The problem was there were two representatives who wanted the job — and their support split the Republicans right down the middle. We'd been in caucus for a couple of hours and had taken a bunch of votes but there was still no clear winner."

"And that's when you stepped in?"

"That when I put my foot in my mouth. I suggested that both sides find someone they trusted and elect that person so that this new Speaker could gavel the House to Christmas Recess. Then over the holidays, I suggested, the two sides would do some horse trading and figure out who was going to get the job. Then the first order of business in the new year would be to officially elect that person."

"That sounds like a reasonable solution."

"Yeah, that's what I thought. The problem was there wasn't anyone the two parties could agree on. Nobody was neutral enough or trusted enough. So, they turned to me. I hadn't make enough enemies and everybody figured they could easily vote me out come the new year if I became a problem."

"And just like that, you were the Speaker of the House of Representatives."

"I took it to be in-name-only — but there's no such thing in Federal Law. So, I was the real Speaker of the House. I didn't think enough about it to even go by and see what the Speaker's office looked like. I caught a plane out of DC and headed home for Christmas."

"We will pick this story up after the break," A.B. Onassis said to the camera. "Stay with us."

CHAPTER 19

Onassis began the next segment by saying, "You took the title — and the job of Speaker of the House because ...."

"All of us wanted to go home for the holidays. The Democrats were hanging around just so we'd have a quorum to officially allow Congress to be on break."

"You didn't even go to the Speaker's Office in the Capitol Building?"

"I didn't see the point."

"What official duties as Speaker did you perform?"

"I simply gaveled the House into Christmas recess."

"Then you flew straight back to Texas — nothing having changed?"

"Well, I did have a Secret Service agent assigned to me who flew to Amarillo with me."

"Were you aware that you were now in the line of succession to the Presidency?"

"Not at all. The idea never entered my mind and no one else said a thing about it."

"Now," Onassis said, adjusting the clipboard in his lap and his position in his chair, "Leo Gibson was President."

"Correct."

"And who was Vice President?"

"We didn't have one. It was President Gibson's duty to appoint someone — anyone he wanted and for that person to be confirmed by the Senate."

"What had happened to Vice President Will Mandel, Gibson's longtime friend and political ally?"

"He had resigned over his part in the Netgate scandal."

"Meaning there was no Vice President?"

"Not at that moment."

"What was keeping President Gibson from naming a new VP?"

"No one really knows. There were rumors that he was considering a couple of different people — but he'd yet to meet with either and certainly had made no nomination."

"Where was the President at that time?"

"He and his wife were enjoying a California vacation at the estate of big Democrat fund raiser and Hollywood producer, Terrance Dymytryk."

"And that's when he had a brain aneurysm and died."

Porter nodded his head.

"The Secret Service," Porter said, "reported that the agents on duty outside his bathroom heard his body hit the floor. He never regained consciousness."

"When did you first learn of President Gibson's death?"

"About 3 A.M., Texas time when three Secret Service Agents, plus the one assigned to me as Speaker of the House, and an Air Force Colonel carrying a briefcase came knocking."

"The briefcase — what we call the 'football' — the nuclear codes?"

"Yes."

"And what did they say?"

"'Good morning, Mr. President.'"

"Must have been a shock?"

"Was it ever."

"What did you do?"

"I invited them in and they explained what had happened."

"Did they give you any options?"

"No. According to the Presidential Succession Act of 1947 in the event of the death of a President and with no Vice President being in place or capable of assuming the office, it falls first to the Speaker of the House and then to the President Pro Tem of the Senate."

"Did you consider turning the office down and stepping aside for the President Pro Tem — who would have been George Tossen at that time?"

"No. I'd spent too much time in the military. When the duty falls to you, you pick up the flag and carry on — no questions asked."

"And so you did."

"Yes."

"Well, now that you've decided to run for the office — because you want the two amendments, the 27th and 28th — the Congressional Term Limits and the Balanced Budget Amendment."

"Correct."

"Aren't both of these amendments already proposed and in discussion in Congress?"

"They've been proposed. But they're both in committees and tabled indefinitely for discussion — where they've been for about the last year and a half."

"You've managed to get them on this November's ballot in every state and territory of the Union."

"I didn't do that alone. Most of what is accomplished by an administration requires the efforts and influence of a great number of people — most of whom will never be known."

"Well, isn't that what you wanted?"

"It is — but there won't be much discussion of either amendment and they'll likely fail in the general election — unless there's someone there to push for them."

"That's where you and former Congresswoman Tracy Holyoak come in."

"That's our purpose."

"I understand you are both getting decent crowds at your campaign rallies so far."

"The turnout has been OK — but it needs to be bigger. So we're keeping at it."

"What's this about a Convention of the States?"

Again Porter sighed.

"After the terrorist attack on the VA hospital in Amarillo, I called Congress back into Special Session to deal with the underlying immigration problems no one in Congress really wants to handle."

"But Congress passed the Tossen/Sturges Immigration Act. It had everything you wanted in it. And yet you vetoed that on national television and called for a Convention of the States. Why?"

"As I said at the time — yes, the things I asked for in an immigration fix were in the Tossen/Sturges Act — but it also violated the Constitution. Congress knew it when they wrote it."

"Why was it unconstitutional?"

"Because it changed the qualifications for citizenship. Those requirements are already enshrined in the Constitution and no bill, no act of Congress can change that. It will take a Constitutional Amendment."

"Another one?"

"There in is my problem. There is too much wrong with our nation as it is that Congress *won't* or *can't* fix because of to whom they owe their true allegiance — and it's not the American people."

"What does that mean?"

"The average seat in Congress pays around $174,000 a year. Yet the average cost of a campaign to win such a seat is now roughly $12 million. How does that compute? Even using the *new math*, that doesn't make sense. So there are other forces at play behind each seat — lobbyists, organizations with agendas, wealthy individuals with personal itineraries — big money groups that want to win and control these seats. The only way that's going to change is to make significant changes to our Constitution — changes Congress on its own will never make."

"But what about the dangers of such a Convention of States. I've read where it would be possible for such a Convention to go wild — become like a runaway jury. They could change everything."

"That's very possible."

"Aren't you afraid of that? What if Socialist or Communist or Fascist elements get hold of such a process?"

"That is a real danger. I admit that. But personally, I have more trust in the American people than I do in politicians. If we can get the right kind of people into such a Convention of States, this could be a very positive thing."

"Right kind of people? Like who?"

"There's no way to specify this, but I'd like to see a Convention of ordinary Americans. I'd like to exclude politicians of every stripe and every level — political activists — lawyers and even doctors. No big business owners, no millionaires or billionaires — no one who has inherited their wealth instead of having earned it. No televangelist — no big church preachers or priests. No college professors. What I'd like would be plumbers, carpenters, electricians, small business owners — people who own shoe stores, sandwich shops, bars — people who have to make their business work, make a payroll every couple of weeks and pay for benefits for their employees. Grade school teachers — not facilitators or administrators — but teachers who buy supplies out of their own pockets to make sure their students get what they need. People who have served in the military and first responders — the kinds of folks who put their lives on the line every day to do the right thing. Small farmers and ranchers — people who make it possible for the rest of us to live the way we do.

"If we could get those kinds of people — I would leave it up to them what it is we really need and what we can do without. That would be an earth shattering convention. These are the kinds of people who know life up close and personal — not from a classroom or out of a book. These are the silent majority members — the forgotten Americans. I would leave the fate of our nation in their hands any day."

"Surely you'd like to require something?"

"Only that they were American citizens, that they read both the Declaration of Independence and the Constitution before they attend the conventions." Porter paused a moment and then added, "And — that the entire convention recite the Pledge of Allegiance to the US. F Flag and say a prayer prior to each session."

This edition of "Liberty, Justice and Onassis" was quickly one of the most viewed programs on YouTube, and rebroadcast by several outlets.

Hard as they tried, neither the Democrats nor the Republicans could come up with a program to equal it. Hollywood stars and producers made slick videos — comics did stand ups trying to mock the idea. All were seen but none even slowed down the growing audience of the "Liberty and Justice" episode. Every imaginable format was tried by every sympathetic channel and host — but it quickly became evident what the public wanted to see and hear.

Attempts were made to hijack the video but they ultimately failed. The word was out for all of those who wanted to hear it.

CHAPTER 20

The few reliable polls, or those thought to be semi-reliable, claimed the presidential campaign was a 3 way horse race. Individual networks, channels, or media source polls always tended to show the candidate they were backing, openly or covertly, to be ahead by clear single digit leads. Contrasting polls told different stories.

To be reliable a good poll had four requirements. A balanced poll took all major factors into consideration — party affiliation, sample size, place of residence and trustworthy polling practices.

First were carefully crafted questions which didn't encourage or suggest the response. There was a real science to this and not all organizations wanted to bother with such niceties. Their polls were taken and explained with goals in mind from start to presentation.

The second requirement was a significant sample size over a large enough area. Too small a sample explained nothing.

Next where the poll was administered was significant. Samples restricted to urban voters in certain sections of the nations were automatically slanted before they were administered.

Factors came down to specifics such as — urban, suburban, or rural

— not polling those who owned property in suburban neighborhoods but who didn't live there — not polling people who lived on the corner as opposed to the middle of the block. History had proven that corner residents thought differently, spent differently, and were different from their middle-of-the-block neighbors.

Finally, good polls were truly scientifically designed and administered. An accurate poll required those who took it to be honest respondents. Random phone calls were more of an irritant to their targets than a source of facts. It was known that people would lie to the caller and give the shortest and quickest answers to questions simply to get off the phone. Mail and on-line polls were so unreliable that no truth seeking pollster would use either form. Most of these requests ended up in the physical or virtual trash. Those who did respond had historically proven to be biased well before taking any poll.

Regardless of their reliability, monthly, weekly, and even daily tracking polls were stories on all newscasts. Smart people paid little attention to them.

※

Porter made the best of any opportunity, except for latenight talk shows, to reach out with his messages. He and Tracy appeared together a few times, and she did her own share of radio, TV, Internet, and print interviews. Their messages were coordinated through the campaign so that they ended up always being on the same page.

This required constant updates to briefing binders they both carried. Material was dated at the top and new material was color coded so that the newest material was easy to spot.

To questions about *"social justice"* the answer was something to the effect that social justice had little to do with true justice. It was often a handle given to the cause of the day. Many of these causes turned out to be manipulated events or misunderstood arrests of identifiable minorities. Tracy and Porter always asked for the facts in the cases and would not deal with the slogan of the day. When they were proven correct in their approach, the media was surprised. For example there was the case of the Hispanic athlete who claimed discrimination for racist tags left in his locker during a game. The culprits turned out to be both an assistant equipment manager and the jock himself. The equipment manager was caught on store surveillance video buying the spray paint. The athlete himself had written a check to the man for the job.

Social justice was, both Tracy and Porter would say, a form of political, racial, or even sexist bias played out to achieve a desired end. When such ends were exposed, they did more harm than good to the people they were hypothetically designed to help. In order for most of these social justice goals to ever be achieved, a great deal of public ignorance was required. For politicians to push these causes, selective ignorance was needed.

Humor was also a factor in Porter and Tracy's ability to get their messages across. Self-effacing lines written by the campaign but based on real life events from the two candidates often proved to be more memorable than any logical or thoughtful argument. This Tracy quickly mastered — in fact, some say she even sounded like Porter in some of her delivery. It was not on purpose. The two were simply on the same page and had the same kind of sense of humor.

THE STONE-FACED SERIOUSNESS OF THE OTHER CANDIDATES OFTEN showed itself in skits which mocked them. But trying to lighten up was more of a challenge than many professional politicians can handle.

George Tossen tried to joke about his being wheelchair bound, but this came off as an unintended slam against others who faced the same affliction without complaint.

On the Republican side, VP candidate Trey Rifkin was much better at humor than Vincent Sturges. It got to the point that Sturges stayed away from humor and let his VP carry that load. But Rifkin, with his white Stetson, didn't have the best timing. Even with some of the best joke writers in the business working for them, sometimes for free, they couldn't help when the delivery was less than stellar.

The Democrats were always waiting for their VP candidate, Amelia Morris, to go off script once she got a laugh. This she did more than once and almost always to a disastrous effect.

INK found that Porter and Tracy were getting more air time than either of their competitors. They spun the story to claim that the media was supporting the Independent ticket.

Lost in all the reports which sprang from that was the fact that the Independents both made better guests than any of their opponents. That was never said or reported but suddenly the public was seeing more and more of both the Democrats and the Republicans. What didn't get reported was that the impact the Independents were having outweighed the amount of screen time they were afforded.

It was like the actor who screwed up every scene he or she was in. This caused the director to have to get the few lines such actors had in a single medium or close-up shot. Such actors were always letter perfect in close-ups. What never seemed to register was that it wasn't face time but the impact, sincerity, and power of presentation which made the difference.

ON THE BOOK FRONT, A NEW NOVEL BY PORTER RANDALL CAME OUT. He had completely forgotten about it. It was a novel he wrote in his down time as a form of relaxation. Ward Adair and Ella Suzuki got wind of it and orchestrated its updated release without Porter's knowledge. He was furious when the book was announced as a number one best seller. Porter never wanted his fiction to have anything to do with his politics. While his campaign managers knew this, they also knew the power and the boost the novel could have in the political race.

Like all his others, this was a medical mystery. The title was, "How To Kill A President." It was not about the assassination attempt on Porter's life but rather about a double agent who had been made Physician to the President. Porter made sure not to make any of the tale too close to what actually had happened to him with Doctor Leonard Millhuff.

Millhuff was the surgeon who operated on Porter on Air Force One after the President had been shot. He had used first Depotherazine and then secretly Mannltol to keep the President in a coma. The events had been the inspiration for Porter's new story, but in this one, an Army doctor with as much experience as Porter had in Afghanistan, was the villain. A hidden side of the doctor's character was subverted and manipulated to the point where he was administering tiny, untraceable amounts of poison to a sitting President. It was a good yarn with lots of inside the beltway intrigue. The doctor wasn't exposed until the last chapter and was a very likable character up until that point.

This offered other opportunities for Porter to be on talk shows without having to mention politics. That, of course, was the plan. Porter finally saw that and agreed to the plan as long as nothing political was to be allowed during any of the interviews.

Both of the other two parties had ghost written books already out — but both were duds. They were too political, too self-aggrandizing, and each had a total lack of humor — something Porter's novels always sparkled with. What truly angered the Democrats and the Republicans was that they'd paid considerable fees for their candidates' books but none ever even broke into the top 20. And there was nothing they could say about Porter's book because the others had been published first — and fallen flat — while Porter's late comer was a spectacular success.

Howard Sterling and Saundra's publisher caught a janitor copying pages of their book. Once in jail the woman revealed she was working for INK. Zeb Tolle disclaimed the woman and no other link, other than her word, was ever discovered. She had been paid in cash by an unknown person. The publisher doubled their security after a review by computer expert Mckinna McPhee. The manuscript itself was locked away in a safe at the end of each day and the authors continued to work.

Their next chapter "Truth Tellers and Scalawags" separated true journalists from those who masqueraded as reporters, correspondents, columnists, cartoonists, photojournalists, anchors and news contributors. These were truly in it only for the bucks, the publicity, and to push their hidden agendas. Howard and Saundra didn't pull punches here. They named names and cited ethics and factual violations of every scalawag they called out. They chose this tag because it so aptly described those who were rats and rascals openly behaving badly. They purported themselves in ways which, when examined, were as harmful as they were amusing and mischievous.

CHAPTER 21

The first debate had been assigned to Public Television. The site was New York and the subject was finance. The lead network anchor, Rachael Eleanor Kensley-Holmes wore her tawny hair in a tight bun. She was dressed in a dark blouse that was buttoned to her throat. It was a long sleeved blouse in spite of it being a sweltering August night outside the New York University auditorium where the event was held. Ms. Kensley-Holmes was small busted and wore a tiny gold chain with an indistinct charm at the end. There was a PBS pin in the lapel of her jacket and the woman spoke with a slight British accent.

She introduced the other two anchors, a male and female reporter before she addressed the audience.

"You may applaud at the end of each presentation and at the introduction of each candidate. Nothing else will be allowed.

"The order of the candidates' introductions is the order in which they will answer questions. Each is allowed 3 minutes to respond and 1 minute to rebut any subsequent questions from this panel. The candidates will not address each other and will only speak to questions posed to them by us."

She turned around to the stage and introduced Republican, 70 year-old, Vincent Sturges, as the Honorable Senior Representative from Ohio. The white haired and bushy eye-browed figure stepped out to applause and took his place at the first podium.

Second Ms. Kensley-Holmes introduced the Honorable Senator George Tossen from California, Democratic Senate Majority Leader. The sixty-nine year old, full chested, Tossen used his strong hands to wheel himself to the center speaker's stand which had been lowered for his height. His blond hair, as always, seemed to be carelessly combed but somehow casually in place.

Lastly Porter was announced as the President of the United States from Texas. While there was applause no louder than that of the others, Porter stepped over, offered his hand to Tossen who seemed shocked but took the outstretched hand. Then Porter shook hands with Vincent Sturges before taking his place at his lectern, the one on the right hand side of the stage.

"Since tonight subjects are limited to financial issues, we will begin by offering each candidate three minutes to make an opening statement."

Although it didn't need it, Sturges began by brushing back a full shock of ice white hair. As he spoke his bushy eye-brows moved to emphasize needed points or simply to draw attention to the candidate's face.

"Our nation faces a national debt beyond what those of us my age could have ever imagined. It has been accumulated under administrations both Democratic and Republican. But we must keep in mind that we have fought the longest war in our history in Afghanistan, as well as the Gulf Wars following the 9/11 attacks. I am not here to argue the need for those expenditures but want to remind you that there are reasons for this debt.

"And yet it is ours to deal with. The best financial minds in the nation are doing battle with this debt and looking at how we can best deal with it.

"As Republicans our path has always been less government and restrained spending, but our efforts along these lines have not done the job. We must do more. Under a Sturges Presidency my first action will be to convene a commission of economic and financial experts who will be given the single charge of devising a rock solid route to our nation's financial solvency. I will not accept any half measures but expect a full and complete solution with steps we can and will act upon immediately to bring our national balance sheet back into the black.

"We are a nation that pays its bills — and this one is no different. We will not just address it but cut it down and down until it no longer burdens us."

The audience clapped politely as all eyes turned to George Tossen.

Tossen just shock his head before he uttered his first words.

"The last time this nation's budget was balanced — and we even had a surplus was under a Democratic administration. Like him or hate him but Bill Clinton did what no one else could do with our country's finances. But having left money in the bank for the following Republican administration, the bills began to pile up and up. Today it is no longer sustainable. We are reaching the point that the interest we pay on the money we have borrowed will equal the money Congress has to spend on all other priorities combined. This madness must stop. And, as in the past, only Democratic administrations can do it. We will also need a supporting Democratic Congress — don't forget that. Together we will rein in this wild spending on needless military advances and immigration projects which never seem to have an end.

"Where have all these great financial minds been these last several years? Why have they not come together before now to give us guidance — and aren't most of these supposed financial geniuses the rich and powerful who have the most to lose if we do put our house in order?

"No, what we need is strong leadership — my leadership — to give our economy the jolt it needs to not just survive but to recover and grow healthy once more.

"Helping the rich get richer is no way to help our struggling nation to learn to stand on its own two feet once more. We all need to tighten our belts — we all have to be willing to take part of the pain. We must not gift our children and grandchildren with the obligation and payments which will not just weight them down but crush them. What we need is strong and knowledgeable leadership. That's why I'm here and offering to serve as your next President."

The applause this time was slightly more enthusiastic but nothing overwhelming.

When Porter spoke, his voice was calm and steady.

"It really doesn't matter whose fault it is that we're in this mess. After a car wreck the first thing you do is stop the bleeding. Blame can come later.

"So how do we stop the bleeding? Let's begin by no longer paying for things we don't really need — like a government supported radio and television service."

There was a noticeable gasp from the audience.

"If you want the programing NPR and PBS offer, pay for them or let advertisers do so. It should not be your government's job to fund what you listen to or watch. And there are other programs just like this one.

"Monty Python once did a skit called 'The Ministry of Silly Walks.' In it the government would provide grants to people who could come up with a silly walk. We don't have that, but we are paying $150,000 dollars to encourage government bureaucrats to practice yoga so they won't get fat? How about a campaign to get the cool hip people not to vape or smoke? Everyone who doesn't know what sitting and smoking will do to their your bodies don't need government help, they need a brain fix — out of their own pocket.

"Why are we paying for a wine making curriculum in community colleges? Don't we have enough people who know how to make wine — and enough winos — already?

"Why are we spending $15 million dollars to study the effectiveness of golf equipment?

"Why are funds for school lunch programs being used for sprinkler systems?

"Why did we build a gas station in Afghanistan that no one uses — to the tune of $45 million?

"And these are the small ticket items.

"Why are we giving foreign aid to nations whose stated goal is to destroy us?

"Why are we bringing in immigrants with no talents or skills and then paying them more each month than we pay our vets or those who have saved and earned Social Security? There are nen with several wives and dozens of children — able bodied men — who never seek a job? Why should they? We are paying for them to own businesses and drive better cars than Americans citizens can afford. Some of these immigrants have no intention of ever becoming Americans — they don't plan to learn to speak English or become a part of our society. They want to rebuild the failed states from which they came on this ground which our men and women have fought and died to protect — for Americans.

"This is the most generous and benevolent nation on the face of the earth. We're the first to be there when disaster strikes — the first to offer help with medication and technology — and yet the first nation to be damned and abused for our help.

"This needs to stop. It is already within the power of Congress to stop all these things — it has been for years — and yet Congress has not and will not — ever do so. We all know this.

"Let's stop accepting the way things are done and demand they be fixed. You can't run your house the way we run our government. This is the reason for the proposed Balanced Budget Amendment."

A warning buzzer sounded in the auditorium. Porter's time was almost up.

"In 1911 Will Rogers told us, 'When you find yourself in a hole, the first thing to do is stop digging.'"

There was a standing ovation that moderators took three minutes to calm.

CHAPTER 22

An unexpected helping hand came to Porter's campaign from a comedy special on Netflix. This one outpaced Porter's Interview with Onassis with its number of views.

It was a stand-up comic/ventriloquist Shaun Pinkus. He was previously known for a bit he had done which became a catch phrase. It was called, "My Smart Phone Must Be The Village Idiot."

Pinkus was 40 with a full head of sun-bleached, dirty blonde hair, dark eyes and a slender nose. The 6 foot 3 comic slouched in his customary black sports coat with matching open collared shirt and slacks. His most popular character was a stuffy college professor, Dr. Sebastian Chatterton.

The Professor, just 4 feet tall, had receding deep brown hair with touches of gray at each of his temples. His slightly oversized head was oval and he sported extremely bushy eyebrows, a slightly bulbous nose that was vainly and red at its tip. His jowls were beginning to sag but gave him the countenance of a no nonsense scholar. He wore a tweed jacket with leather patches on the elbows. Additionally he had half-glasses which hung on a cord at about the third button of his pastel oxford shirt and old school tie. His slacks were pressed — his wingtip shoes were polished.

Las Vegas was the site of the videoed clip, although it wasn't evident from the background. The set appeared to be the lost baggage collection shed of some major airline.

"Good evening, Professor," the comic said once the puppet was seated on a high stool beside him.

"Mr. Pinkus," the professor responded in a deep, slightly raspy smoker's voice.

"Before we begin, I must tell you that the management has requested that we keep our comments G rated."

"Young man, I'll say any damn thing I want in whatever vernacular I feel to be appropriate. I've earned it. I have tenure."

"What exactly does that mean — tenure?"

"It means I am a scholar and a gentlemen. I've publish numerous articles in prestigious academically credited journals, three books, and I'm in demand for speaking engagements — not unlike this one. That means I am a professional and have the right to exercise my total academic freedom without censorship or interference from any asinine administrator."

"Well, Professor, we're not on campus now and the management here —"

"Can suck lizard eggs through a plastic cholesterol straw."

"They just don't want us to use words like — like — say ones that begin with 'f' and end in 'u-c-k.'"

"What in the hell is wrong with *firetruck*?"

"Then words like — 'ass' —"

"Asinine? Ass happens to be in The Bible — more than firetruck."

"Let's say they want us to use — decorum."

"Do you even know what decorum is, young man?"

"Certainly, I do. It means using manners, proper etiquette and good taste."

"No, it doesn't. Decorum is an ancient art and craft form of engraving certain types of glasswork using gold and silver. Its roots and world class artisans were and are in Turkey."

"I didn't know that."

"Let's not go down that library aisle — what you don't know. We'll be here all night."

"All right. Tell us about today's college students.'

"They get dumber each year."

"You can't mean that?"

"I think most of them got in on rowing scholarships while the only thing they know about a boat is how to sink it."

"That's rather harsh."

"Today's students are only interested in getting drunk and getting laid."

"Well, in their defense, when I was their age that's pretty much what was on my mind."

"And look how you turned out."

Pinkus made a face and looked away from the professor as the audience roared.

"I'll have you know, Dr. Chatterton, that I was originally an aeronautical engineering major. I wanted to design airplanes."

"What happened?"

"I flunked out after two semesters. Couldn't do the math."

"So the system does work."

"Are today's students interested in politics?"

"As long as they think it's a way of getting them something for free."

"And do they understand Socialism?"

"They don't understand Daylight Savings Time."

"But Socialism sounds so good. Free college, free health care, social justice, free —"

"That's where it breaks down."

"Where?"

"Free. What's free?"

"Everything, they say."

"From whom?"

"The government?"

"I ask them, "In order to pay for all of these *free* benefits — you need money — real money. What does the government create that makes money?"'

"They can't answer that?"

"They can't begin to answer it. The only money any government ever has is the taxes it collects from people who live under its system. So, I ask them, 'What if you create something amazing — marvelous — earth shattering — with the doodling you're doing right now while you're supposed to be paying attention to this lecture? Do you think you're going to suddenly get rich? Think again. According to Socialism, you didn't build that. It doesn't belong to you. It belongs to the government. What money you do get will be taken up in the taxes you'll have to pay to support the free *stuff* for everyone else."

"And what's their response to that?"

"They say they'd move. I ask to where? They say to somewhere that isn't Socialist. That's when I point out, this is proof of what British Prime Minister Margaret Thatcher once said. The primary flaw of Socialism is — 'Eventually you run out of other people's money.' That's when students cool off on Socialism."

"Would you classify your students as primarily liberal or conservative?"

"I would classify them as *Animalia Chordada Perissodactyla Equus Africanus*. Thought to be extinct. But they're not."

"Could you make that a little more down to earth for those of us who are not so — educated?"

"The universal *Dumbasses!* That's what they are. But it's like climate science — you believe what you want to believe — the facts be damned. The average IQ would require negative numbers to be properly quantified."

"Is it true that today's students have a difficult time with essay questions?"

"They have a difficult time with the English language. Spoken, written or emojied."

"What about you, Professor? Are you political?"

"I try to understand the issues. And I vote. But deep in my heart I feel that voting for a politician is just a way of encouraging them."

"You don't think much of politicians?"

"There are three professions where you're paid to lie — weather forecasters, lawyers, and politicians. Politicians just get to steal more."

"Did you come from a politically active family?"

"As I recall my mother was a Democrat — as my father used to pronounce it, the emphasis was on the '*dim.*' My father was of the total opposite opinion — he was a Republican. As my mother used to pronounce it, "a *repulse-ican.*"

"What is your heritage?"

"As a child I remember my mother calling my father a "prickly pear." Although now that I think back on it, perhaps she didn't really say the 'pear' part. And she may have pronounced 'prickly' a little differently."

"And your mother?"

"Father often said my mom was an A-number 1, world class Birch."

"And you? How are you registered?"

"Plywood."

CHAPTER 23

The lone vice presidential debate was held two weeks later. There were few fireworks. However, it was all but impossible to deny that Tracy Holyoak had bested her two opponents. Amelia Morris came off as being knowledgeable on most topics but seemed at sea when in-depth follow up questions were directed at her. Republican Trey Rifkin was never flustered from his years speaking before Congress. It was evident to even the most casual viewer that he strung together long used catch phrases and party talking points to field unexpected questions by the panel. In the final analysis Rifkin's performance didn't seem totally at ease.

The ratings of this debate were less than half those for the first Presidential Debate. Not much was expected nor delivered by those in the number two slot of each party.

Tracy did her best to keep the two proposed amendments front and center in all her answers. Both Morris and Rifkin had to weave and dodge to keep from dealing with that aspect of the race.

THE NEWS OF THE WEEK CAME FROM A PODCAST WHICH REVEALED A

George Tossen aid had been in secret meetings with Chinese authorities. The topic of the discussions was reported to be a way to accommodate the Chinese. Their ham-fisted method of controlling news and access to the topics on the Internet was significantly less flexible than the US approach. New technology was making the need for hard-wired connections less important and therefore less controllable. In the end it was believed that no agreement was reached and that China was determined to go its own way. They would attempt to block outside sources and create their own Internet.

The fact that a candidate for US President was willing to accommodate such ideas was a deep cut to the Tossen movement. The central issue was Tossen's stake in several technology companies and Internet outlets after the Netgate scandal from years before. He had not been implicated in that fiasco but was certainly taking advantage of financial possibilities in the aftermath. Other Democrats came out against such an accommodation ever being made by the US — or even discussing it.

The Tossen camp at first denied such a meeting ever even happened. Their tune changed first when photos of the airline ticket used appeared. Then it was altered once more when video was produced of the Tossen aid entering an official Chinese government building. Tossen claimed that he had always been willing to talk with any nation about any topic. Yet, he said, he held the US's interest first and foremost in his mind. He also pointed out that he was certainly in no position to do any kind of negotiating with China or any other foreign government.

Next there was evidence of contributions to Tossen's personal foundation/charity. It was to the tune of several hundred million dollars. The campaign then stopped trying to address these issues at all.

⚜

HOWARD AND HIS CO-WRITER, SAUNDRA, FINISHED THEIR MOST difficult chapters and wrapped up their book. It was now in the publisher's hands for the most part. As the pair reviewed the galley prints of the manuscript, they found themselves amused. There were still minor miswordings and grammatical mistakes even the copy editors had missed. Over all they were very pleased with what they'd achieved with the book.

It was the, "You never told me that," and the occasional laugh or even gasp from Howard's wife Jessica which always found Howard and Saundra exchanging glances and smiles. Jessica had never read a word of the book as Howard and Saundra pounded it out — 6 days a week, every week. Few in the public had any idea how smart or perceptive a woman Howard had found in the beauty he married. But he never failed to appreciate her intellect and observations. Hers was not a mind to be ignored.

The world largely saw Jessica as arm candy for the very few public outings the Sterlings had made together over the years. They never guessed at the pride he took in her well beyond her external appearance.

"What about the actual printing?" she asked without looking up. "When does that begin?"

"Tomorrow," Saundra said.

"It will be bound and shipped in a little over two weeks," Howard said.

"Not like the old days," Jessica said picking up the next set of galley sheets.

She had written her own book, "In Front of The Camera and Between The Shots" about the real life of a cover model. The book was a best seller, but she always claimed it was because of the collection of pictures in the center section rather than her words.

She may have been right at least on some level. Jessica had a captivating face, a lovely figure, lustrous hair, and flawless skin. None of her attributes she ever took credit for —well, except for the starvation diet she suffered to keep her figure. She called herself a freak of nature which the distorted lens of a camera happened to like. Her words of wisdom to future models were to not even read their own press releases much less believe them.

"If someone succeeded in the artificial profession of modeling," she wrote, "their time would likely be short, the temptations enormous, and the likelihood of self-destruction magnified beyond belief. No one deserved to see themselves as an exception to the truths of life which they shared with everyone who walked the earth. And the biggest danger," she said, "was to somehow consider that they deserved the praise and adulation heaped on them. A model is the result of an accident of genes, DNA, as seen through the refraction of light and the twisted effects of pieces of ground glass — the camera lens. Be the person you wished other beautiful people truly were but rarely proved to be."

She was amazed and appreciative of what Howard and Saundra had achieved in their work. There was no doubt in her mind that the work would have far-reaching effects and would become a classic for years to come.

Howard added something to a blank page.

"What's up?" Saundra asked.

"I've decided to add a post script to the book." Howard continued to write and after he looked it over, he handed it to his co-author.

She read: "You can tell real journalists by their souls — the soles of their shoes. If they are worn, you're dealing with a real reporter who chases down leads. Journalism is not a desk job. It's a pounding-the-street/chasing-down-leads profession. Go seek the truth."

Saundra liked what she saw and was nodding her head when Howard said, "I never found a place to add this. So I thought the very last page of the book would be the place."

Without responding, Saundra picked up her pen and wrote something more to the page. When she was finished, she showed it to Howard.

It read: "Don't get hung up on chasing a story — chase the facts. It's too easy to fall in love with a storyline, a narrative, and then spend your time searching for facts to support it. Journalism works the other way around. Follow the facts — they will lead you to the true story."

They then showed it to Jessica. She reached over and borrowed Saundra's pen. She circled Saundra's paragraph and inserted it into Howard's before his last two words and then added a few words.

The final product read like this: "You can tell real journalists by their souls — the soles of their shoes. If they are worn, you're dealing with a real reporter who chases down leads. Journalism is not a desk job. It's a pounding-the-street/chasing-down-leads profession. Don't get hung up on chasing a story — chase the facts. It's too easy to fall in love with a storyline, a narrative, and then spend your time searching for facts to support it. Journalism works the other way around. Follow the facts — they will lead you to the true story. Go seek the truth — leave the storyline, the narrative to fiction writers."

Howard smiled as did Saundra when she read it. Saundra took her pen back from Jessica and signed her name under the paragraph. Howard did the same and the book was done.

CHAPTER 24

Porter was fully at war with Congress and with lobbyists and professional politicians whose life-blood depended on the wild west of Congress as it existed. No one in political power wanted a new sheriff in town nor true law and order in their business. He lost the support of his few fans in the Republican party and any of those even remotely connected with Congress.

One columnist suggest that Porter and Tracy should drop the theme from "Smokey and the Bandit" and substitute "You and Me Against the World."

Ward Adair and Ella Suzuki relished the underdog position and did everything they could to capitalize on it. In their view it only helped Porter and Tracy's image with *"ordinary Americans."*

A couple of polls bore this out, but Porter didn't put any more faith in these than any others. Except for occasional trips back to DC to meet with visiting heads of state and taking care of other presidential business, Porter and Tracy stayed on the road — or more aptly, in the air. Porter, of course, had Air Force One, but the plane the party had supplied for Tracy was a well appointed and comfortable ride. Neither Ward nor Ella knew the name of the person behind the plane but all were grateful for it.

Between rallies, Porter and Tracy did Skype and Facetime interviews with TV and radio stations near and far away. Meanwhile the campaign worked on the social Internet media. They also produced hundreds of thousands of yard signs, rally posters, and mailers which were daily spread across the nation.

One of the most unique interviews Porter did was with three college students on a nationwide university-only Internet hookup.

❦

THE VIDEO CONFERENCE WAS WITH PORTER IN HIS AIR FORCE ONE Office wearing a blue windbreaker with the Presidential seal on the breast. He was on a flight from Alaska to Hawaii when the Internet conference began.

Each of the interviewers sat around the edge of a wooden table in short arm chairs in what looked like a college board room. The three had name plates in front of them printed in large black letters on folded paper.

The center participant was a slightly heavy set coed, Perla Powell, who had close cut eggplant colored hair, and dangly earrings. She was braless and had breasts which moved with every motion of her body as seen through the multi-color LGBTQ tee-shirt.

To her right was a young man named Edwin Crane. He was a 19 year-old young man, healthy looking but not particularly athletic. He had Rastafarian brown hair and an attempt at a beard which wasn't working. He wore a pale green Oxford shirt with the collar buttons undone and a fraternity pin on his breast pocket.

On the far left end of the three was another young woman, Aura Kohl. She had black hair in a page boy cut with bangs down to her eyebrows and black eyes. The rest of her hair was cupping her round face. She had a tiny diamond in one side of her nose, full lips and a willowy body with a long white neck. She wore a baggy gray sweatshirt with nothing on it.

"Good afternoon — and good morning to some of you," Porter spoke first.

"Mr. President," Ms. Kohl said.

"Hi," Ms. Powell seem to say reluctantly.

"Good day, Sir," Edwin Crane said.

"Let's begin. Who has the first question?" Porter asked.

"I do," Perla Powell asserted herself to take charge. "What is your position on the LGBTQ movement?"

"Mostly observational," Porter said. "I am an outsider who doesn't have anything for or against it."

"You could be a member?" Ms. Powell shot back.

"I belong to way too many organizations as it is. And I think given the position I'm in, I don't think its wise for me to join organizations in which I have no stake."

"So you're saying you don't support LGBTQ?"

"I did not say that. Neither did I say I was in favor of it. All I really know about the LGBTQ movement is what I've seen, heard, and read. Nothing, so far, has encouraged me to deny it nor to give it my personal nor professional endorsement."

"If you're not for us, you are against us!"

"That's not a very good recruiting slogan. There are a lot of people who may or may not be in the closet, as well as their family and friends — who don't find themselves moved by what they've seen from the LBGTQ community. You're not helping your cause by chasing people away simply because they're not onboard. There really are people who are totally neutral."

"What have you seen from our movement which offends you, Mr. President?"

"Overt displays of public affection. Rioting. Belligerent Gay Pride parades. Intimidation to anyone who criticizes *anything* done or said by the organization. A person should be able to express an opposing idea without the LGBTQ mafia coming down on him or her like a hammer."

"So you think we should stay in the closet?"

"Once again, I didn't say that. Why are you so intent on alienating someone who isn't against you?"

"It doesn't sound like you are for us."

"There is more than black and white — right or wrong — for or against. I don't want to preach to you, but when Jesus was told of a person casting out demons in His name — the apostles tried to stop him and Jesus said, "Do not hinder him; for he who is not against you is for you."

"You are preaching at me."

"I'm sorry you feel that way. But you wanted my honest opinion and I gave it to you. I believe some people are born gay or homosexual — and I think there are those who are drawn to that lifestyle because of events in their lives. They are not for me to judge — and I don't. Biologically, I don't believe there are more than two genders. But I do think the government has no business in anyone's bedroom — and it shouldn't be trying to control the way we think.

"It's also my opinion that the LGBTQ community does itself a lot of harm in its in-your-face tactics. In a land of freedom and liberty you should be able to live your life your way with or without my blessing. What I don't get is the support your movement gives to other movements, which, if they came to power, would throw members of your group off of roofs and stone them to death. On some matters I feel we should all live and let live."

"Then I'm afraid, Mr. President, you are a homophobic bigot."

"That seems to be a LGBTQ's default position. If someone is not 100 percent on board with any and every manifesto, slogan, thought or musing of anyone in your group, rather than try and talk to them your approach is to label them. Label them with the nastiest thing you can come up with and then dismiss them as worthless and irrelevant. Even friends sometime disagree with each other. Since you will not allow even discussion, much less disagreement, your movement is totalitarian. As long as it's *'comply or die"* you'll continue to make more enemies than friends.

"Do we have another question?" Porter said before Ms. Powell could continue with her prepared talking points.

"I do, Mr. President," Edwin Crane said. "Do you think the voting age should be lowered to 16?"

"Do you remember when you were 16, Mr. Crane?"

"Yes, Sir. Those were good days."

"What were the main things on your mind in those days — your sophomore year in high school?"

"Pretty much what they are now?"

"Girls, parties, and video games?" Porter asked.

"Well — yeah, that — and skateboarding back then. But I also think I was old enough to vote then just as I am now."

"How many amendments are there presently to the Constitution, Mr. Crane?"

"Twenty — two," he said looking at the two women on the panel with him for assistance.

"Twenty-seven," Porter said. "Who did we fight in the Spanish American War and where did we fight?"

"Why are you trying to give me a history test?"

"You want the power to control and even change history. Those who don't know their history are bound to repeat it. Do you want to contribute to that?"

"I'm not a history major. I'm into engineering. And I'm on the golf team."

"Golf. And engineering. What kind?"

"Nautical. I want to build ships?"

"Do you want to repeat the mistakes that caused the sinking of the Titanic? If you don't know why it sank...."

"An iceberg — and compartments that weren't truly watertight as they were supposed to be."

"Excellent. You do know your history there. But would you vote to get us into a war over a mishap that was nobody's fault?"

"Of course not."

"How can you be sure if you don't know what happened back then? It might happen again."

After a moment Porter said, "For your information we fought Spain in both Cuba and in the Philippines. And the war was started because the USS Maine was sunk in the harbor of Havana. Historians now tell us it was not because the ship was attacked but because of something gone awry with the unstable munitions of the day. There was an explosion in the ship's ammunition's storage locker. It was a war that didn't need to happen."

Porter looked to Ms. Aura Kohl as he asked, "Do you have a question for me, Ms. Kohl?"

She had papers before her as did the others but she didn't refer to them.

"What is your position on Socialism? You must know that a large majority of college students are in favor of it."

"I do know that. What is your major?"

"Art history."

"And your future plans?"

"To go to a good graduate school and get a teaching job at a good university."

"And you want to do this in a world that isn't fair to everyone?"

"Well — yes. But I want to be a fair teacher to all my students."

"How do you get into what you call a '*good*' graduate school?"

"By having good grades."

"What's your grade point average?"

"Four point zero."

"Excellent. Mr. Crane, what's yours."

"I've got a solid 2.8."

"Ms. Powell?"

"Two point five."

"Ms. Kohl, it doesn't appear that all the students — even here — are equal. If Mr. Crane is going to follow his dream, he'll have to go to a '*good*' graduate school. Ms. Powell, are you going to graduate school?"

"Law school," she said.

"It appears everyone here isn't equal — even right here, Ms. Kohl. I figure you spent a lot of time studying — not going to parties — not attending other fun events — but then that was a decision you made. No one forced you to do that. And you are now what we might call a one-percenter. How many of your grade points are you willing to give up to Ms. Powell and Mr. Crane — and others — so they can be equal to you. It will help them to get into '*good*' schools after they finish their undergraduate work?"

"Well —," she stuttered a moment "— none. I don't owe anything I've earned to anybody else."

"But it would make everyone equal. So what if you have to go to a lesser graduate school — and end up teaching at a lesser college —

wouldn't you feel it's more fair to help your fellow students out — even those who don't work as hard or study as hard as you do?"

Ms. Kohl shook her head silently.

Porter asked her another question. "Who or what part of the government in Washington do you trust to decide how much of what is yours is really theirs — and everyone else's?"

After a moment she burst into tears as she left her chair and hurried off camera.

CHAPTER 25

INK and most other progressive media led their news the next day with either a headline or a graphic freeze-frame of Ms. Aura Kohl leaving her chair and the words "President Bullies Coed." Other headlines read: "President No Friend Of LGBTQ" and "Only History Majors Qualify To Vote At 16."

Only WOLF TV went to the trouble of tracking down Aura Kohl and getting a statement from her the next morning.

"I was shocked," she told the reporter. "I'd always thought of myself as liberal and even a Socialist. President Randall made me suddenly confront my stupidity. I work and study hard to make something of myself. I'm the first one in my family to even go to college. What kind of system would take away what I had earned and give it to someone on the golf team or someone who never cracked a book all semester? I realized I have many things I thought I believe which I need to re-examine. It hit me like an electrical shock."

The off camera reporter asked, "How do you feel about the President?"

"I thank him. He made me think — not always an easy thing to do when you're as stubborn as I am. He's got my vote."

The other candidates tried to make as much of the President's interview and the fleeing young woman as they could. However the interview video with Ms. Kohl was out there and two days later the story was dead.

Zeb Tolle stormed around his office in the INK Tower as his building was known in New York. The 40 year old, wooly-headed multi billionaire didn't look fashionably unkempt but used and almost homeless.

Gathered in his office were all his senior producers and editors.

"Look at our stock!" he shouted pointing to one of three Wall Street visual tickers at one side of his desk. "I couldn't give this thing away if I wanted."

"Zeb," Merlin Laszowski, the thick but somehow regal network Executive Producer was the only one in the room with the nerve to speak up. "As I remember it, you didn't buy this network for profit — but for influence."

"And what kind of influence do I have with it now?"

"Did you succeed with your first computer program? When you wrote it, did it work exactly as it was supposed to without a single glitch?"

"Glitch? This is fuckin' more than a glitch. When I bought this thing, it was number 1. Now we don't even make some of the lists."

"My question is, when you had problems and things went to shit in your garage workshop, did you quit? Or did you go back and rethink the whole thing until you found the problem."

"That's why we're here at this very moment!" Zeb pounded on his desk.

"What did you do when you found that your basic idea wasn't correct?"

"Merlin, are you telling me I'm wrong?"

"I'm only asking the question no one else will. You can fire us all right now. Just like you did with Howard. So, do we tell you the truth — what you need to hear and hang on as the ship goes down — or do we say what you need to hear."

Zeb didn't know how to vent this anger at hearing these words. His face got so red that his old acne scars were visible. But instead of letting it out, he stormed out of his own office.

The top execs at the network looked at one another and then at Merlin.

"What did you expect?" Merlin said. "We're just a rich man's toy. He wants to play in a game he knows nothing about. He's not going to cool off and come back with open arms and an open mind wanting to know what we really think."

The room was silent as all the news execs took this in.

"Right now, the only one he's angry with is me. My advice, if you want it, is to get to work on your resumes and put out feelers. We're not going to get better. INK will never again be what it was. And Zeb Tolle didn't get rich by doing what others advised him to do. He goes his own way. Right or wrong he has chosen the path he wants to follow — and the path he expects us to follow. I've been with this thing since it started — and I think I'll go down with it. That doesn't mean I won't try to change our course — but you've been here long enough to know how Zeb works. We may hold the only light going down in this rabbit hole — but don't expect much to change."

He looked around the room at friends and professionals he'd worked with for years. All their heads were hanging dejectedly toward the floor.

"If any of you want a recommendation from me — you've got it. But I've lost as much credibility as the network has. My word might do you more harm than good — but feel free to put me down as a reference. I couldn't speak higher of any of you than I can today. You tried to do your job — but now you are seen as Nazi troops who claimed they were just following orders.

"Go do what you have to do. This is my fight — my fight to lose, I'm afraid. But much more than any of you, I helped make this bed. I'm a dyed-in-the-wool liberal — always will be. So part of this is my following my politics instead of my professional ethics. Don't you make the same mistakes.

"I'd suggest you tell any possible employer that you've learned a lot here — but a lot of what *not* to do. Now, go."

In the news media as a whole it was evident that the Independent ticket was gaining support with the public. No matter how individual outlets felt about either of the other two parties, it became evident that the real fight was against Randall and Holyoak — not between the Democrats and the Republicans. This resulted in toned down attacks on anyone other than the Independents.

Rallies for both Tossen and Morris or for Sturges and Rifkin always seemed to compare well with those of the President's or Tracy's rallies. Only a rare shot revealed that the crowds in the Democratic and Republican rallies were all pushed forward and made to imply that the events were crowded. The exceptions were pictures shot from the rear of a stadium, coliseum, or events center that exposed the fact that many of these rallies were half full at best.

The Chinese scandal was quickly lost in most of the media reports. Once again Tossen was framed as a new FDR — the only things missing were the glasses and the cigarette in a long holder. Amelia Morris had been convinced by her handlers that she was just a face, an actress playing a part. She stuck to her scripts and learned to pay attention to any information supplied to her with pictures and footnotes. She would have a bigger part to play when she and Tossen were the winners, she was told.

As the campaign wore on, the problem with Vincent Sturges became that his true self was coming through. Word was leaking out about how he was treating those around him — he was often compared to Hillary Clinton. For years Sturges had been a glad-handing, always smiling, folksy guy who came across as someone anybody'd like to have a beer with. But Vincent never was that. He thought himself superior in intellect and power to those lesser than him. He knew he was born to lead but within a representative republic, it was always the case that he had to whoo those who needed him but weren't wise enough to know it.

Trey Rifkin stood up to the riggers of the constant demands on his time. He had the ability to cat nap and always came across as fresh and thrilled to be with those who turned out for events.

Vincent was not happy when campaign advisors tried to give the vice presidential candidate more stage and air time. Sturges was wise enough to see how people were reacting to his partner, but his jealousy would not allow him to yield to what was best.

On the Independent side, Tracy Holyoak was enjoying the rally events more than she ever imagined. When she and Porter appeared together, she tried to give him the spotlight. It was Porter who demanded that she share the space and time with him. They made an excellent team. At times they were even able to joke with each other unprompted. The audience felt as if they were in on real moments — which, in truth, they really were.

Ward Adair and Ella Suzuki kept working the behind the scenes events and kept both positive and negative polls away from Porter and Tracy. The campaign team was always afraid of over confidence but came to believe in their candidates unlike any had ever done before. Running a campaign had been merely their life's work and neither party nor candidate made much difference to them — it was always the challenge of winning which drove them. This time was so much different.

Unknown to anyone, the campaign heads had even found themselves falling in love with each other again. They both had such a knack and a love for the challenge of their work that they operated in complimentary spheres of their own. Now that they were working towards the same goal and even allowing themselves to believe in the cause for which they worked, everyday seemed to be a sunny day full of laughter, bright people to work with and untapped energy.

Even Grant Yarbrough found a new zest for politics. As campaign spokesman he was getting time in the sun and on all the media outlets — and he found he wasn't as interested in skirt chasing as he once was. This surprised him but he didn't feel deprived. What did surprise him was how his mind kept turning back to Therese Herzog. She was the 36 year old presidential speech writer he had last seen when working in the White House. He found excuses to video call with her to make sure he was employing the correct verbiage Theresa had actually used. Thus words from Porter's speeches appeared in current party press releases.

Theresa with her round glasses, pale, grey eyes, curly chestnut hair was not anywhere close to the flashy women Grant had been drawn to before. But the Ph.D. in Communications had long been secretly in love with Grant. She had thought him out of her league. As it was turning out, politics was making for strange bedfellows — especially when the campaign bounced back to DC occasionally.

CHAPTER 26

The second presidential debate was staged in Denver. The refurbished Paramount Theater at Glenarm Place downtown in the mile high city had a capacity of 1,700. It was filled and had media standing all around the edges as the network hosts took their places.

This event was granted to three different commercial channels and each sent their most popular anchor to be part of the questioning panel. From the layout on stage it was clear that the Democrat's George Tossen has been given the last place as the lowest lectern was on the right. It was unknown until the candidates were introduced that Porter would be in the first place on the left.

Again Porter made a point of shaking hands with each of the other candidates as they entered and each tried to appear their jovial and congenial best for the debate.

"Tonight's topics are all limited to social issues," Keith Brissett the ABC host announced to the audience. "Each candidate will be given 3 minutes to respond and 1 and a half minutes to respond to follow up questions from the panel."

The newsman had a long face with a short carefully styled deep brown beard, hazel eyes and an appealing smile. "This is not to be an audience participation event, so please be respectful and gracious to each of our candidates. The ballot box is the proper place for you to express your support for whomever you choose — not here." He turned around to face the candidates and then nodded to the woman to his left as he said, "The first question comes from Cabbott TV's morning anchor, Leanne Dubois."

The black woman had full deep red lips, and wavy black hair above her subtle loop earrings. She had the kind of face millions of Americans had come to love with their morning coffee over the past two decades. Her voice was clear and almost melodic.

"The nation still seems divided these days," she began, "over the question of abortion. Please tell us about your position."

"Thank you, Ms. Dubois," Porter said to the debate hostess and then he looked up at the audience.

"While Roe vs. Wade is settled Supreme Court law, I, like many in this land feel it is a subject in which the Federal Government has neither a place nor a voice. My reading of the Constitution finds no mention of any reproductive rights among our rights to life, liberty, and the pursuit of happiness."

There was some scattered applause but it did not interrupt Porter nor draw the attention of the host.

"From my most basic understanding of human biology, it takes two people to create a third. Back when I was a teenager and we could laugh at such things, there was an old bumper sticker which read, 'If you drink, don't park. Accidents cause people.'"

This got a good chuckle from the audience.

"But this is no joke. The creation of another life is not something anyone should ever take lightly. Unfortunately, we know too many people still do. And there is the issue of rape. That particular part of the question I believe needs to be addressed separately.

"The basic issue is not just a woman's issue."

This brought out a few boos from the crowd.

"While biology makes it the woman's charge to carry a new life — somewhere, unless there is a star in the East, there's a father. If he is not man enough to step up to his duty for this new life, there is a place for the law to intervene. By this I mean more than child support.

There is also the obligation of full and complete fatherhood. We are all familiar with the fate which often falls to fatherless children.

"But there is a third life involved — a life without a voice — too often without the hope of liberty or the pursuit of happiness — or even life.

"To me, this, as I said, is not an issue for the Federal Government. Let's get the government out of our bedrooms. This question is one which, I believe should be left to the individual states and to the people there. As the Constitution says in the 10th Amendment, 'The powers not delegated to the United States by the Constitution, nor prohibited by it to the States, are reserved to the States respectively, or to the people.'

"So, I see the abortion issue as one that can be easily addressed. We should ask, 'At what age do we feel it should be legal to murder a child?'"

There was a solid round of applause for this.

When Porter said no more, Ms. Dubois asked her follow-up question.

"President Porter, you do admit that Roe vs. Wade is settled law, by our highest court, do you not?"

"Yes," Porter said. "But so was Dred Scott — "referring to the Dred Scott vs. Stanford case of 1857. In that instance a black man sued for his freedom and that of his wife and two daughters. The Supreme Court ruled 7-2 against Scott. The court found that neither Scott nor any other person of African ancestry could claim citizenship in the US. Therefore Scott had no court standing to bring suit in Federal Court. Scott, his wife and children were determined to be the property of his owner. "Had we let Dred Scott stand, Ms. Dubois, where would you be today?

"And how about Prohibition? The Supreme Court is made up of human beings who can and have been wrong in what they decide.

"Regardless of how you couch the issue of abortion — as a woman's right — as a pro-life issue — it still comes down to the elimination of a human life who has no standing in court to even ask for life. No matter whether a child was conceived because of drink, drugs, lust, stupidity, or even a mistake — a life has begun and should not be ended for the sake of convenience, embarrassment or as the only answer to a problem which need not ever have happened."

When it was their turn, both Vincent Sturges and George Tossen spoke their party's line. They used the expected platitudes and talking points with neither of them offering anything new.

The next issue of the night was support for Planned Parenthood.

CHAPTER 27

Senator Tossen took the first question on Planned Parenthood — which was really an extension of the first. He and his party were, as always, fully in support of the organization. He had numbers and facts to support his position. Vincent Sturges had facts and numbers, too, only his position was opposite from the Democrats.

When it came Porter's time to respond, he said, "Here's the rest of the story.

"The leading cause of death of Americans under the age of 50 isn't car accidents, heart disease, cancer, drug overdoses, or gunshots — it's Planned Parenthood. Last year by their own figures, Planned Parenthood performed 330,000 abortions. That's death by abortion.

"As an organization, Planned Parenthood has over $1 billion in net assets. Back in 2014 their data proved that Planned Parenthood's revenue exceeded their expenses by over $90 million. Simply put, they don't need our tax dollars. They are a for-profit organization getting non-profit status and unneeded tax funds. Taxpayer funding of Planned Parenthood equals more child murders and fewer adoption referrals.

"Planned Parenthood provides more abortions than any other provider in the nation. One out of every four abortions in the US is carried out in a Planned Parenthood facility.

"Recent undercover footage revealed Planned Parenthood employees in several states who were willing to help and assist in human sex trafficking of girls as young as 14. Only one employee was fired for this practice. The truth is, Planned Parenthood is not a safe space for women, babies or young girls.

"Contrary to what they would have you believe, Planned Parenthood does not provide mammograms at the majority of their facilities. And it is not a significant primary care provider to women, either.

"The business model of Planned Parenthood focuses on abortion. The more child murders the more income.

"And there are more than a thousand federally qualified health centers in the country. These facilities provide sexually transmitted disease testing, cancer screenings, contraception and primary care. Planned Parenthood is never the only option.

"And lastly," Porter began as the warning buzzer sounded, "Margaret Sanger, the much revered founder of Planned Parenthood, was a strong believer in the practice of eliminating unwanted traits and even races. She once said, 'In the example of the inferior classes,' — meaning blacks, Hispanics, and even Catholics — '...the most merciful thing that a large family does to one of its infant members is to kill it.'"

***

VINCENT STURGES HAD A PREPARED JOKE ABOUT EDUCATION FOR THE last subject. Rehearsed as it was, the joke fell flat. This was the sign of what came with the rest of his presentation. The sum total of his argument was that education was an expensive undertaking and needed a complete Congressional overhaul.

When the panel turned to George Tossen, the Democrat wanted more government funds directed to education. In his eyes all the problems with education could be fixed with more money and more government guidance. Additionally Tossen promised free college education to all if elected.

Porter was shaking his head as he listened to his challengers. Once it was his turn, he began with, "The word 'education' is not in the US Constitution. Anywhere. Education is not on any list of enumerated powers for the government. It's none of the Federal Government's business. It was the Carter administration which separated Education from Health and Welfare. Today it is a stand-alone cabinet level department. US education standards have tumbled and our children have been getting dumber and dumber since that time.

"When government is involved in education, it is no long education but a population control program. Education by government is little more than mandatory propaganda of children from kinder through higher education. Education should be controlled as close to the families which have children in these programs as possible. It should not be run by government functionaries far away from the classrooms. And it should not be in the hands of bureaucrats who neither know nor understand the needs of local school districts — nor of colleges.

One of the reasons for the Balanced Budget Amendment is because there are parts of the government that are too expensive — and don't work. We spend over $100 billion each year on 4,000 employees and programs like Head Start and The School Lunch Program. And by the way — we wouldn't feed our troops some of what's in these School Lunch Programs.

"You will notice that neither of my colleagues," Porter gestured to Tossen and Sturges, "ever claimed any positive results for the government's interference with education — because it doesn't exist. Not that achieving positive results has ever been a criteria for any government program.

"We spend more on education in this country than any nation in the world — and how do we rank? Just looking at industrialized countries — we are pretty much in the middle of the pack. Sixteen other nations outrank our students in science and 23 score better than we do in math. Is that the results we should expect from all the money poured into education since 1979? Not by my measure. We should have seen massive improvements — not the middle of the pack.

"So why continue year after year doing what doesn't work?

"Look at Common Core — there's a disaster that continues to get worse. We've gotten revisionist history out of it and standardized tests most members of Congress couldn't pass.

"And let's not forget the failures of the soul-crushing programs of No Child Left Behind, Race to the Top, Head Start, and Every Student Succeeds Act. We don't allow students to fail — no one gets below a C no matter how much or how little they've done to deserve it. If you can't fail, you can't really succeed. And we put the blame on the over-worked, underpaid teachers who have to labor in the salt mines of classrooms packed with far too many pupils — many of which can't speak English or understand the teachers.

"What's happened to the home front? Parenting used to be a major part of every child's education. No more. We drop children off at the school with no sense of discipline and proper behavior — because they don't' learn it at home. Yet, we expect the teachers to do it all. There's no longer any concept of personal responsibility.

"The rich and the privileged pull every string they can to get their children into college. Schools some would never qualify for on their own. Why, because they know all colleges are not the same — and they know neither their family nor their children have done the work to get into better schools.

"The government wants to be able now to track our students' every move, every grade — which will all be passing grades — and put that into a national data base — to be used by whom — and for what? Can we just trust the government on this? I don't think so.

"DC doesn't want you to be able to pick a better elementary, middle or high school for your children — particularly when you and I both know there are charter schools out there which leave public schools in the dust. But if you choose charter schools, the government loses control of their education — just as they do with home schooling.

"And whose bright idea is it that *everyone should go to college?* I'd rather have my car fixed by a good mechanic than by a Ph.D. in gender studies.

"When did good honest work become something shameful? I had a friend whose father was an attorney. His father was doing so well he decided to add a private bath to his office. He called in a plumber who did an excellent job. But when the attorney looked at the bill, he couldn't believe it?

"'Look,' he said, 'I'm a lawyer and I don't charge this much an hour.' The plumber just smiled and said, 'When I was an attorney, I couldn't either.'"

The point was made and this got a good laugh.

"We need people with skills and the willingness to do the dirty jobs that make this world go around. We owe a big thank you to Mike Rowe for introducing us to hundreds of these people over the years.

"Don't let any of us think we are better than those who do jobs we won't or *can't* do. No degree, no amount of classes or diplomas will make you a smarter or better person. We all know some good people who barely have enough common sense to cross the street.

"We all need each other and should be thankful for anyone who does an honest day's work — regardless of their level of education.

"Basic education is needed by all of us. It's what you might call a process of catching up with the human race. But when the students are unwilling and the parents are not interested or leave it to the government, we'll end up with cookie cutter people who all think the same and — guess what — vote the same. I wonder if that's the real goal?"

CHAPTER 28

The October Surprise is a political device each party has used over the years to derail the opposition. While many believe it's a relatively new phenomenon, the tactic dates back to the 1830's. All campaign managers and operatives know the history of this maneuver and how it has worked over time. There were lessons to learn from each.

In the 1838 election then President Martin Van Buren was involved with the first one. There were federal prosecutors who were planning to charge top Whig politicians in New York. The charge was labeled as a *"most stupendous and atrocious fraud."* Truth was both parties were involved in the whole thing.

The scheme was to pay Pennsylvanians to cross state lines to New York and fraudulently vote multiple times in the election. The prosecutors, who were members of Van Buren's party, didn't announce any charges until mid-October. The point was to maximize the indictment's electoral impact. Democratic newspapers of the day leaped on the story. They ran sensationalist headlines like, "*Sound the Alarm. Your Liberties Are In Danger*" and "*A Gigantic Plot to Elect Harrison By Fraud.*"

Of course, the Whigs denied the accusations. Then one of the voter-fraud's organizers admitted the charges. Surprisingly the average elector's reaction was not what the Democrats nor Van Buren and the Republicans had hoped. The public simply assumed that this was just the Democrats up to their same ol' shenanigans. Van Buren lost the election by six points but only one member of the Whig party was ever prosecuted.

On October 20, 1880, the New York Truth newspaper published a three-sentence letter purportedly written by Republican nominee James A. Garfield. The note, addressed to a man in Massachusetts, reportedly vowed support for Chinese immigration to the US. Additionally, the letter contained the opinion that employers had the right *"to buy labor where they can get it the cheapest."*

In those days there was widespread support for restricting Chinese immigration by both the Democrats and the Republicans. Even Garfield had expressed such views.

At first handwriting experts were slow to authenticate the letter as having come from Garfield. But the letter was on government stationary. And, too, the man to whom the letter was addressed was never found.

Garfield was in no hurry to react to the scandal and only beat his opponent by .02 percentage points in the popular vote. He did lose California, the state most impacted by Chinese immigration.

Following the election, the letter's author turned out to be a New York newspaper journalist for "Truth." The reporter was arrested and indicted for fraud.

The famous *"Rum, Romanism and Rebellion"* October surprise happened in 1884. It involved Republicans who accused Democratic candidate James G. Blaine of running a campaign based on alcohol, Catholicism, and the Confederacy. Later Blaine claimed he never heard the initial charge made against him at the parties' nominating convention. Although Blaine won the GOP candidacy, he lost the election because of public furor over the suspected campaign foundation. Blain lost thousands of votes from anti-prohibitionists, Roman Catholic immigrants, and southerners. New York Irish in particular voted against Blaine, and he lost the election to Grover Cleveland.

Then there was the 1920 claim that Warren G. Harding had *"negro blood"* and that FDR was gay. The false charges against Harding came from a known racist professor at Wooster College. Harding's advisors had to prove his European heritage.

Franklin Roosevelt, Harding's opponent in the race, had been assistant secretary of the Navy. He had authorized an investigation of homosexuality at a naval facility in Newport, Rhode Island. Members of the investigative team were directed to participate in homosexual acts in order to gain firsthand evidence that would stand up in court. When FDR heard about this, he slammed the investigation shut.

Still charges of FDR's sexuality were made but never proven. And in the end, Harding won the election.

In 1940, Roosevelt already President for two terms, was considering a third term run. The US was not yet in the European war. At home FDR came under pressure from African-American leaders for the military's continued segregation. His opponent in the general election was Wendell Willkie, a Republican with a strong civil rights platform.

To mitigate the political damage, Roosevelt responded with his own October surprise. He promoted Colonel Benjamin O. Davis, Jr. to Brigadier General — the first African-American to reach that rank. FDR also announced the creation of the Tuskegee Airmen — what became World War II's famous group of African-American military pilots.

L.B.J.'s 1964 election looked like a disaster when senior aide Walter Jenkins was arrested for disorderly conduct with another man in the Washington DC YMCA. The Toledo Blade called the incident "*...so notorious a gathering place of homosexuals that the District police had long since staked it out with peepholes for surveillance.*"

It only took 2 days for an FBI insider to leak the story to the Republican National Convention. The GOP was happy to take the story and run with it. In what looked to be an election-sinking scandal, the Jenkins incident vanished from the front pages. In its place was the news that Soviet Premier, Nikita Khrushchev, was ousted from power by his hardliner colleagues in the USSR Then the People's Republic of China conducted its first nuclear weapons test. Republican Barry Goldwater's own hardline approach suddenly seemed like a path toward nuclear war. In the election, President Johnson won in a landslide.

The October Surprise of 1968 began with L.B.J., who had decided not to run again. But he did call a halt to the bombing of Hanoi. Hubert Humphrey was glad and very supportive of an announced last-minute peace deal. Johnson had tried to arrange an end to the war between the Viet Cong and the South Vietnamese.

Efforts through back channels supposedly encouraged the South Vietnamese to withdraw from the talks three days before the US election.

Nixon won the election.

Then in 1972 Richard Nixon tried to announce a peace agreement with North Vietnam in Paris. But suddenly the North Vietnamese pulled out of those talks.

National Security Advisor Henry Kissinger was rushed to Washington from the peace talks and announced a press conference on October 26. The South Vietnamese accused DC of duplicity in the negotiations, and the North of being out of step with the US. At the scheduled news conference, Kissinger proclaimed that *"peace is at hand."*

The announcement pushed Nixon further ahead in the polls and enabled him to win the election with 60 percent plus of the popular vote. Still, it took 2 and a half more years for true peace to come about.

President Jimmy Carter's earlier bold but failed attempt to rescue the captives didn't help his image nor his election chances either. Carter's later efforts to free US hostages from Iran militants cost him the election with Ronald Reagan. The reason some claim, was that Reagan made a secret deal with the hostage takers not to release the captives until 2 days after the election.

The 1987 Iran-Contra affair almost cost Reagan re-election. The deal was that the US sold arms to Iran and used the funds to fight the anti-Communist militia in Nicaragua. The affair did hurt George Bush in the '92 election between Bush, Clinton and Ross Perot.

The 2000 George W. Bush race with Al Gore had the October Surprise of Bush's D.U.I. arrest 24 years earlier. Some strategists believed the news, first reported by Fox, and it cost Bush 5 states. However, he won the election after a Florida recount.

When in 2004 Osama bin Laden claimed responsibility for the 9/11 attacks on New York, this made him a villain. And Bush, who bin Laden called a dictator because of the Patriot Act, only gained support and won his re-election.

But Bush was very unpopular by 2008. The Republicans picked as their candidate for the next election Senator John McCain. But when McCain couldn't remember how many homes he owned, he doomed his own candidacy. No regular American would ever have such a problem.

This teamed with the stock market's crash in '08 and growing joblessness — at a 14-year high — make McCain appear out of touch. He returned to the Senate after losing badly to Barack Obama.

The 2012 surprise was a secret video tape of Republican Mitt Romney speaking to what was supposed to be a private high dollar fund raiser. It cost him his election when it was released that October. The words that damaged Romney were, "There are 47 percent of the people who will vote for the President no matter what. All right, there are 47 percent who are with him, who are dependent upon government, who believe that they are victims, and who believe the government has the responsibility to care for them."

The surprises of the Clinton-Trump elections were several. The Democrats would claim the Republicans and Trump in particular had colluded with the Russians. Hillary Clinton smashed e-mail device and, Bleach Washed the hard drive of an illegal computer she secretly maintained in an unsecured bathroom closet. When WikiLeaks founder, Julian Assange, produced over 3,000 supposedly *"missing and unrecoverable"* emails, the Republican October Surprise brought her down in a contested race.

Even Leo Gibson, the President whom Porter replaced, had his October Surprise. He figured out that vague innuendoes were more effective than facts. So he let word slip out that his opponent was a possible rapist. The story was that his Republican rival, Felix Oliver, was the unproven culprit in a college rape case. The real story was that Oliver and members of two other fraternities had conducted an old fashioned panty raid on two sorority houses. While women's lingerie was the only thing taken, one coed claimed to have been held down and raped. The supposed offender had used a condom and left no DNA evidence behind. The police could never pin the event on any group much less an individual. Oliver's fraternity claimed the dorm where the crime took place was not the one they raided.

The popular story on campus was that the young woman, a student from a very strict religious family, had lost her virginity at a party only nights before and concocted this tale to cover up her lapse in morality.

Since the story was never proven or disproven and no one was charged, there was no proof positive that Felix Oliver was not, in fact, the rapist. But everyone who knew him swore he would have never committed such a crime.

The ploy worked and Leo Gibson became president — only to die in office a little over half way through his first term.

Thus when the second Randall-Sturges-Tossen debates ended in early October, everyone awaited this year's first shoe to drop. What unexpected October Surprise was waiting in the wings — or would one of the combatants somehow do themselves harm?

CHAPTER 29

In Syria where the caliphate of ISIS was being pounded into defeat day by day, a US Army Captain, Ivan J. Noon, was brought up on murder charges for the killing of three Syrians in a small village. The story was a worldwide headline, and the Army was in full cover-your-ass mode from the first moment of the arrest.

Still on the campaign trail, Porter heard about the incident and after talking to brass in the Pentagon, he asked to speak to the senior Army commander in the field. It took a half hour to arrange a satellite phone call to Major General Seth Brackenbridge. The general identified himself as soon as he was on the line. "What can I do for you, Mr. President?"

"I want the story behind Captain Noon — the unvarnished, down and dirty story."

"Yes, Sir. Capt. Noon was on vehicle patrol, which was on his own initiative — he likes to be where the action is — where the danger is. The second vehicle in his convoy had been torn almost in half by an IED — we suspect an 80 mm shell rigged and set off remotely.

"What was left of the convoy went into a defensive position. The bodies of the dead and wounded were being recovered and helo transported to the nearest evac hospital.

"The village had settled down even though our people were ready for anything. Local villagers had begun to go about their business on foot and in their carts and wagons.

"Three men, Syrians, were walking past the wreckage. Capt. Noon thought he recognized one of the three as a known teenage bomb maker. The kid had a distinctive limp we'd seen before. Without warning the captain pulled his .9mm pistol and killed the kid before he shot and killed the two men with him."

"Did anyone else around participate in the incident?" Porter asked.

"No, Sir. To all the other soldiers it appeared the captain had just gunned down three civilians in cold blood — which turned out to be the case — in a way."

"The men killed were not ISIS fighters?"

"Well, Sir, they were — as it turned out — and they were all armed. But they were just walking by — they were noncombatants at the moment.

"According to Capt. Noon," the general went on, "he knew the limp and even the clothes the teenager was wearing from surveillance footage we had. He thought the three were there to see how well their bomb had worked first hand."

"But," Porter asked, "they *were* ISIS?"

"Yes, Sir. No question. They have been identified. And it seems that the kid was some sort of electronic genius — if he'd ever had a chance to go to school. He learned bomb making from his father. The kid got his limp when one of daddy's bombs went off in the family basement."

"Where is Capt. Noon at this moment?"

"Under heavy guard in a solitary confinement cell. He has been charged with triple murder."

"General," Porter said, trying to control his rage, "get your exec or highest ranking N.C.O. on the horn with us right now."

A moment later there was a click and the General said, "Sir, Col. Kate Dewey is on the line with us."

"I'm here, Sir," the officer said.

"Colonel, you are a witness to the orders I am about to give General Brackenbridge."

"Understood, Mr. President."

"General, I want all charges against Capt. Noon dismissed — immediately. For God's sake, we sent all of you there to kill and wipe out ISIS. It seems to me that's exactly what he was doing. Those SOB's had just set off an IED. As far as I'm concerned, they'd fired the first shot. They were not non-combatants.

"I want Capt. Noon restored to duty — field promoted to Major — and given a Bronze Star with v-device for valor. Captain Noon acted when no one else did. This is an order from your Commander-In-Chief. Do both of you understand?"

The General said, "Charges dismissed, Capt. Noon restored to duty, promoted to Major and awarded the Bronze Star with v device."

"That's what I heard, too, Mr. President," the exec officer said.

"Refer any question about this order straight to me — not up the chain of command."

"Yes, Sir."

Porter then called his Secretary of Defense, Victor Chesterfield. In his Pentagon office, the completely bald, rimless spectacles wearing Secretary sat clinching an empty pipe between his teeth. The man had intelligence, the savvy, and an iron will. He was a Congressional Medal of Honor winner from Vietnam. Victor was one of the few people in the nation's capital Porter trusted completely. The President explained his actions.

"This decision falls on no one but me. Is that fully understood?"

"Yes, Sir."

"Have your shop draw up a press release — and I'll deal with the fall out."

"Will do, Mr. President. This is a good call I believe.

AT HIS NEXT STOP, PORTER ANNOUNCED HIS DECISION TO THE world at a rally in Salt Lake City, Utah. The thunderous applause lasted a full five minutes.

The Democrats and the Republicans, however, were sure Porter had shot himself in the foot with this. They put pressure on their supporting media to push the narrative they wanted.

Some reported that the President had condoned the murder of a teenager by an Army officer. Others decided to stress how the President had exerted his authority before any proper legal procedures could be taken. A few told the story of a President who was quick to act and protect US soldiers in need.

The surprise was that in the early polls they showed an overwhelming support for the President's efforts.

By a full week later, it was evident that the President's military decision had no major negative impact on the campaign. So, another planned October Surprise was launched by the opposition.

From a so-called *"reliable"* but unnamed source, the story broke of a known felon working in the White House. The narrative initially was vague but did identify a *"well known"* person in the President's White House living under an assumed name to cover up a felonious past. Later reports narrowed the person to the White House Communication Office.

Porter and his people were completely caught off guard with the report — which was one of the major intents of the tale. In the air between El Paso and Austin, the President took a call from his White House staff.

"It's me they're talking about," Cinnamon Higdon told Porter. "It's only partly true, but you need to know the whole story. It's something I should have divulged when you first came into office. It's my fault you're in this position. I have my resignation letter already prepared."

"Fill me in first," Porter said.

Cinnamon gave the President the full story. Porter told her, "I never want to even see that resignation letter. Let me handle this. I have a rally in Houston, one in Austin, and one in Ft. Worth. Then I'll be back in DC. Don't you say a thing about this — to *anyone* — until I'm there."

"Yes, Sir, if that's the way you want to play it."

"It is."

As Air Force One continued on its flight plan and the President conducted his planned rallies in Texas, he had his Chief-of-Staff back in DC putting together the facts. Ward and Ella were brought into the loop, and the President explained how he wanted it handled.

All day the story grew and commentators trashed both the President and the felon in the White House. Only a very few outlets remained suspect of the story and covered it with questions instead of accusations and commentary.

CHAPTER 30

Two PM the next afternoon the President stepped into the White House Press Room and took the podium. The reporters got to their feet and then some began sitting before the President said a word.

"I didn't invite anyone to sit down," he said in a harsh and commanding way. "You don't own any of those seats."

When all the reporters were back on their feet, the President looked over the crowd with what could only be described as a scowl.

"Most of you people should be hanging your heads in shame. Not all of you — those of you who are guilty know who you are. You have disgraced yourselves and your profession.

"The press and the media had been called "*the fourth estate*" because of your power to reach and influence the public on matters of national importance. Our founders had enough respect for journalism that they included the need for a free press in our Constitution. What they expected was an honest, fair, equable, balanced, just and objective press. Anyone looking at what we have today can clearly see that such hope has been almost totally dashed. With very few exceptions, you and the organizations you represent are a stigma on what should be one of the primary pillars of our Republic."

Porter paused to let his words penetrate even the most biased journalist in the room.

"By now you know the full facts of this *'felon in the White House'* bullshit. And feel free to quote me on that.

"The story most of you have not told — or the one you have deliberately misrepresented — or out of stupidity repeated without doing any investigating — is the story I will tell now. Don't let anyone be fooled into believing that *"you were just doing your job and didn't know the full story."* You knew what you wanted to know and ignored the facts.

"First of all, the unnamed White House felon is my Director of Communication, Ms. Cinnamon Higdon. You don't need to act like you're writing it down — you already knew that.

"When she was 11 years old Ms. Higdon — which incidentally is her mother's maiden name — was known as Cinnamon Combs. Her mother was Sugar Combs and her two older sisters were Ginger and Thyme."

The President paused and then continued. "Her father, Tyrone Combs, was a failed musician turned petty criminal and drug user. He was a mean drunk who abused his wife and daughters.

"It was Cinnamon and her mother who came home from grocery shopping one evening to find that their father had killed the two eldest sisters — Ginger 15, and Thyme 17. In a struggle with his wife and Cinnamon's mother, Tryone was killed with his own pistol.

Cinnamon had picked it up from the floor when her father dropped it. The child gave the weapon to her mother. Suspecting that both she and her daughter would be charged with Tryone's murder, Sugar took her only remaining child and they fled. For four months they were able to go undetected until they were identified and arrested in the Florida Panhandle.

"Why did they run? Why didn't they turn themselves into the police? They had reported the husband and father's abuse several times but the local police did absolutely nothing about it. It took two weeks for the police to determine that the father had murdered his two eldest daughters. Forensic evidence proved he had been killed in self-defense — by whom it wasn't known. The mother and her last remaining daughter stayed hidden out of fear.

"Put yourself in either of their places. What — exactly — would you have done?"

For several moments there was nothing but silence in the press room. Finally the President continued.

"When Sugar and Cinnamon were located, they were arrested and returned to New Jersey. Within days they were both cleared of any charges. At that point they were no longer felons. It was then that her mother and Cinnamon changed their names — legally — to Higdon.

"Cinnamon graduated high school with an A+ average. She was a National Merit Scholar. She went to college in Indiana and was admitted to Stanford Law School on her own merits.

"She was working in the campaign for my predecessor, President Leo Gibson, when her flair for communication was noticed. She was tapped to come to the White House in a low level position before President Gibson died.

"I am proud that I spotted her talent and placed her in her current position as Director of White House Communications."

Porter scanned the room again. His mouth was firmly set and his jaw tight.

"This lady has been nothing but helpful to each and every one of you in this room — and to so-called journalists across the country — even when she knew you were dishonest and weren't looking for the truth but for dirt on this administration. She's done her job here with nothing but grace, devotion, energy and truth. She does not deserve to have been treated the way you have trashed her.

"When I stop speaking, the White House Press Office is closed to all of you — for at least the next three days — and I don't give a damn what the news is — you'll get nothing from the White House. And you can do your reporting from outside the fence. When we do reopen the office, there will be new rules in place and every one of you will need to be re-accredited. If you can't pass muster, you will be A-N-E on these grounds." The media understood A-N-E to mean "*Absolutely No Entrance.*" Your name and face will be added to the A-N-E list at each guard post.

"So how do you earn back your place here? Some of you *never* will. For those who do — first of all you broadcast or publish this press conference in its entirety. Secondly, you apologize on air, in print, or on-line, whichever is your medium, and you will do so until you have equaled the amount of time and/words you've devoted to reporting this lie — which you knew was false. And lastly, you will individually apologize to Ms. Hidgon — in writing.

"Now, if you think you can take me to court on this — go ahead. As I said, we have changed the rules which govern press access to the White House. They are not written in stone and you have no input into them. There are only a certain number of seats in this room — and neither you nor your organization own any of them. There are hundreds of other real journalists who would just love to have one of these seats.

"So go ahead and take me to court. By the time you can get some liberal-progressive judge to grant you an injunction, you won't be able to reach me. It just so happens I won't be here for the next few days and there will be no news coming out of the White House.

"Clean up your act, people! Do your damn job! And try putting yourself in the place of the innocent people you so carelessly attack with your deformed sense of what your career is supposed to be!"

With that the President left the Press Room.

❦

AN UNEXPECTED SURPRISE CAME DURING THE "*THREE DARK DAYS AT the White House*" as they became known, It was the release of Requiem for Journalism by Howard X. Sterling and Saundra Fontan. The book dropped like a bomb and the media, already back on its heels, was stunned.

Howard and Saundra were the most in-demand guests on radio and TV talk shows. The timing of the book's release was fortuitous and was like a one-two punch with the President's now famous remarks from the White House Press Room.

In the book Howard and Saundra divulged material available to the media but largely unused or ignored — and memos from the likes of INK CEO Zeb Tolle — instructing producers and editors how to cover certain stories and what facts to ignore. They also included transcripts of Howard's newscast violating such memos.

What turned out to be the most significant chapters were chapters 13 and 14 — "The Clinton-Obama Cabal." In it Howard and Saundra listed the scandals and produced available facts and documents. These were the evidence which filled in many of the rumors of unchallenged corruption of both Presidents and their families. The Clintons were first but the lists overlapped.

The book addressed:

— the Monica Lewinsky sex scandal which led to Bill Clinton's impeachment

— the Lincoln Bedroom/ Asia fundraising scandal which saw more than 4 dozen people convicted in the scheme

— Hillary Clinton's private emails where hundreds of national secrets were leaked

— Whitewater, the large savings and loan failure in which several people went to prison

— Travelgate, the firing of the career travel office in the White House to be replaced by cronies who over-charged for government travel

— Pardongate, the first time political donations were connected to presidential pardons

— Foundation favors, evidence showed that the Clinton Foundation was a pay-to-play back door to the State Department, and even an open checkbook for foreigners to curry favor

— Rose Law Firm Records, Hillary's former law firm where missing records were recovered

— Filegate, the Clinton use of FBI files to dredge for dirt on personal and political enemies

— Web Hubble, the sudden resignation and the first imprisonment of a Hillary Clinton former law partner

— Waco, the over-reach and lethal exercise of government police power against a religious cult where 76 people were killed

— the Swedish slush fund, a $26 million overseas account with suspected Iran sanction free passes

— Troopergate, Arkansas State Troopers who helped Bill Clinton set up and conduct affairs with women while he was Arkansas governor

— Gennifer Flowers, the Arkansas news anchor who confessed a 12 year affair with Bill and claimed he told her Hillary was bi-sexual

— Boeing Gate, the contributions made to Bill after he was out of office to get Hillary's help as Secretary of State to obtain a lucrative Russian contract

— Larry Lawerence, a heavy Clinton donor, who was buried in Arlington National Cemetery without any war experience

— Clinton's Speeches, the over-the-top payment to both Clintons for speeches

— China Gate, the transfer of classified US technology from 1994 to 1998 in a wristwatch

— Pedophile ring, the using of underage children of both sexes.

The chapter dealing primarily with Obama began with the *"birther"* controversy, and listed the scandals of the Obama years

— Fast and Furious, the government gun-running scheme which resulted in the killing of a US Border Patrol agent

— IRS Targeting, the singling out of Obama enemies for unjust financial treatment

— Benghazi, which was both an Obama and a Hillary Clinton failure to protect American personnel at the US embassy and then trying to deflect blame for the attack on an unrelated anti-Muslim video

— Obama White House phone tracking, the targeting of Associated Press reporters

— James Rosen, the naming of a Fox news reporter as a criminal because of his reporting and the monitoring of his emails and phone records

— Secretary of H.H.S. Kathleen Sebelius, payment or donation demands from companies her department regulated

— Pigford, the Agriculture Department efforts to compensate black farmers which turned into a gravy-train to many who didn't qualify for any aid

— the General Services Administration, the funding wastes of 2010's training conference held in Las Vegas, to the tune of $823,000

— the Veterans Affairs, $6 million on 2 Disney World conferences

— Solyndra, the poster-child green energy company the Obama administration funded even though it was already headed for bankruptcy

— the New Black Panthers Affair, the Justice Department used a racial double standard by not pursuing claims in Philadelphia of voter intimidation

— unconstitutional acts, Obama, a supposed Constitutional scholar, violated both the spirit and the letter of the law by waging war against Libya without Congressional approval

— the "Dream Act", Obama's end-runs around Congress by dictating which immigration laws to enforce by acting when Congress did not pass laws to enable the result the then President wanted.

With the extensive footnoted and copies of documents as proof of statements, the book was a sellout and into its second printing by the end of the first week of release. The evidence the public had so long craved and had seen only in bits and pieces was now in an authoritative book.

Being so well loved as Howard was, and as on-camera savvy, his and Saundra's interviews drew large ratings.

The Democrats tried to put distance between them and both their former Presidents and Hillary Clinton, their failed presidential candidate. But no one was Teflon enough to withstand these facts from America's once *"most trusted voice in the news."*

While the Republicans rejoiced, they still had the problem of Vincent Sturges' veneer wearing thin. Daily his authenticity was brought into question. At least he learned not to try and tell jokes.

CHAPTER 31

Ward and Ella had their own October Surprise planned. This one was unlike any others in history. It was positive.

Back in February, before the big snow storm in DC, Porter and Deidra hosted an event in the White House. On the invitation lists were all the cabinet members, as well as key members of Congress, and the Supreme Court and all their spouses. The occasion was billed as a celebration of all the *elected* presidents our nation had had.

The meal was followed by a live concert by the country/bluegrass group, The Arkansas Travelers.

This was in keeping with a tradition which dated back to the days of George Washington in both New York and then in Philadelphia.

A portable stage became part of the East Room after it was donated by the Harkness Ballet in 1965. This troupe performed for the Kennedys.

"We're from the Ozarks," the stand-up bass player, Rodney Pollard, said after they'd finished their first number. He was an averaged sized man with a short beard. The whole group wore jeans and boots along with plaid shirts.

"Where we come from, there ain't no Internet and we don't have video games. Folks there are pretty much self-taught. That's how each of us learned to pick and sing. Course, there were folks around home who kept telling us 'As long as you keep pickin' them things, they ain't ever gonna heal.'

"We paid them no never-mind. See, music is one of three things our people make back home.

"The second is shine. And some of that's pretty good — unless you are unlucky enough to get a bad batch."

The banjo player suddenly broke into a complicated and lightning fast break while wearing a screwed up face with his eyes rolling around and around in his head. As quickly as he started, he unexpectedly quit.

"If you get some bad shine," Rodney Pollard said with a straight face gesturing toward the banjo player, "that's what happens.

"We don't go to school much back in the hills. Most of the boys quit right after attendance was taken. We spent most of our growin' up years fishin', huntin', and sometimes watchin' the girls skinny dip down at the ol' swimmin' hole. When a boy grows up enough, he jumps in and joins the girls.

"That's how I met my girlfriend. When I thought she was gettin' fat, her pappy suggested we get married. It was a formal wedding — her ol' man had painted his shotgun white. Then when my bride's water broke, I discovered the third thing we make back home. Turns out we're pretty good at it. We've made 5 already — and we're workin' on 6 and 7 right now. The doctor says we're goin' t' get a two'fer this time.

"Our next song is called 'Salty Dog.' Our manager says most people don't know what some of our songs mean. When he booked us for this gig, he told us to just tell you all that the song is about cigars and interns — whatever that is."

The group began the song while the audience laughed.

Later in the concert, The Arkansas Travelers had an unexpected gift for President Randall. It was a custom made Gibson Mastertone 5-string banjo. The instrument came with red, white, and blue mother-of-pearl inlays on the neck, and the Seal of the President of The United States on the inside of the resonator — which was visible through the clear plastic banjo head.

The President and First Lady were invited up on stage by the group. The President slipped the shoulder strap over his right shoulder and fitted a set of finger picks to his right hand. Rodney Pollard, the base player, stepped up to the microphone again.

"The President and First Lady have agreed to — uh — 'participate' — isn't exactly the right word — it's more like they're willing to be *implicated* with us in a couple of songs."

The audience found this amusing.

"As you might be able to tell from the amount of equipment on stage with us, we are being recorded tonight — and not just by the NSA.

"If you're interested, when you hear any of this again, you can be assured that what you hear will have been heavily edited, remixed, and augmented like hell."

The crowd loved this and both laughed and applauded.

"The point is, if you can remember where you are seated, that's where you'll be on the CD."

This got a laugh, too.

"The first number we're going to do — Rodney looked over at the President who shrugged his shoulders — let's say *'attempt'*..." Porter nodded his agreement. "...is an ol' banjo and guitar favorite called 'Wildwood Flower.' But we're actually going to — attempt — a Woody Guthrie version of the tune using his lyrics and chorus. It's a World War II song — you *do* remember World War II — it was in all the papers?

"This song is 'The Sinking of the Reuben James.' The song tells the story of a US Navy destroyer, named after a Boatswain's Mate Reuben James. He distinguished himself fighting in the First Barbary War. As you'll remember from your US history, President Thomas Jefferson sent US Forces against Muslim merchant pirates and the Mediterranean slave trade of Algiers, Tunis, Tripoli, and Morocco."

Rodney paused a moment as he scanned the audience before he said, "You *do* remember that don't you?"

After another pause Rodney turned to his band mates and said, "We've got to start playing to smarter crowds."

This line got a big but somewhat embarrassed laugh.

Rodney just shook his head saying, "All I'm saying is it's like they say, those who don't know their history are bound to repeat it. Maybe I don't need to tell you that — but then maybe I do." He sighed deeply in exasperation.

"Anyway," he continued, "The USS Reuben James was a convoy escort for US ships headed to Great Britain in October of 1941. At daybreak on the 31st, she positioned herself between an ammunition ship and a known German U-boat hang out. She took a torpedo meant for the merchant ship and went down in the waters off Iceland in about 5 minutes."

Rodney stepped back and Porter stepped forward as he began a banjo rift of the intro. He then sang,

> "Have you heard of a ship called the good Reuben James,
> "Armed by hard fighting men both of honor and of fame?
> "She flew the Stars and Stripes of the land of the free
> "But tonight she's in her grave at the bottom of the sea."

THE REST OF THE GROUP AND DEIDRA JOINED IN SINGING HARMONY for the chorus which began with,

> "What were their names,
> "Oh, what were their names?
> "Did you have a friend on the good ship Reuben James?"

FEET WERE TAPPING AS THE SONG WAS SUNG AND PORTER TOOK THE lead in the bridge with some unexpected banjo picking.

The surprised and delighted audience stood when the number was over.

Next the group sang a song which was written in 1882.

"Proving," Rodney said, "that just because something is old doesn't mean it's no longer worthwhile. I believe many of you here tonight, both in Congress and on the Supreme Court, can attest to that."

Good natured laughter made Rodney hold until it subsided before he said, "Now, I caution you — listen to the lyrics and not your dirty mind. This is a clean song."

The song was "Sweet Violets."

Again the President began with a plucky little rift joined in by Rodney on the guitar and the mandolin player before the President began the song.

"Sweet violets
Sweeter than the roses.
Covered all over from head to foot
With Sweet violets.
"There once was a farmer
Who took a young miss
Out to the barn where he gave her a...
Lecture on horses and eggs
And told her she had such beautiful...
Manners, which suited
a girl of her charms.
A girl he'd like to take in his...
Washing and ironing and then
if she did,
They could get married and have lots of...
Sweets violets,
Sweeter than the roses.
Covered all over from head to foot
With Sweet violets.
The girl told the farmer he'd better stop.
She called her father and he called a ...
Taxi and got there before very long
Cause someone was doin' his little girl...
Right for a change. So he told the farmer,
'Son, if you marry her, you're better off...

Single. Because it's always been my belief
That marriage will bring a man nothing but ...
Sweet violets
Sweeter than the roses.
Covered all over from head to foot
With Sweet violets.
The farmer decided he'd wed anyway.
And started in planning for his wedding...
Suit, which be bought for only one buck
But then he found out he was just out of ...
Money. And so he got left in a lurch ...
A standin' and waitin' in front of the ...
End of this story which just goes to show
All a girl wants from a man is his
Sweet violets
Sweeter than the roses.
Covered all over from head to foot
With Sweet violets."

The song delighted and amused the crowd to their feet once more.

The last song Rodney Pollard introduced saying, "There's likely not a more American song than this one about a fur trapper who fell in love with the daughter of an Algonquian Indian chief. Story is about how he plies his canoe across the expansive river to get to her. It's called 'Shenandoah.' That was the name the French traders first gave to the river we know today as the Wide Missouri."

The song began with a haunting fiddle and guitar intro of the tune everyone in the house knew. The President and Deidra began with a lovely harmony that surprised the audience.

"O Shenandoah,
I long to hear you

> Away, you rolling river.
> O Shenandoah,
> I long to hear you.
> Away, I'm bound away
> Cross the wide Missouri."

Rodney and the rest of the group chimed in until it sounded like a choir.

> "O Shenandoah,
> I love your daughter,
> Away, you rolling river.
> For her I've crossed
> the rolling water.
> Away, I'm bound away
> Cross the wide Missouri
> For seven years
> I've been a courtin'
> Seven years,
> You rolling river.
> Seven more
> I longed to hold her.
> I'm bound away
> Cross the wide Missouri."

The bridge featured a short and melodic lead from Porter on the banjo. The instrumental break also included beautiful guitar, mandolin, dobro, and fiddle additions which made for a hauntingly beautiful song.

The final verse seemed to linger longer than the applause.

> "Farewell,
> my friends,

I'm bound to leave you.
Away, you rolling river.
O Shenandoah,
I'll not deceive you.
Away, I'm bound away
Cross the wide Missouri."

IN DOING THEIR HOMEWORK FOR THE CAMPAIGN, WARD ADAIR AND Ella Suzuki discovered the performance and the recording which was planned for a Thanksgiving release. They had discussed it with the record label and convinced them to move the date to the middle of October.

The CD was called, "American Classic." The cover photo was a collection of shots of the five members of The Arkansas Travelers sitting in a red and white, top down 1957 Chevy Bel Air convertible. On the dashboard stood a small statue of President Randall playing the banjo.

All three songs featuring the President and the First Lady became the number one requests on local and satellite country and bluegrass stations across the nation.

Both the Democrats and the Republicans howled at the timing of the release — but they had nothing to counter the music with. The fact that the music was recorded long before Porter had any notion of running for President didn't make any difference to his opponents.

Ward and Ella also arranged to have The Arkansas Travelers be the opening act of the President's rallies once the CD was released. They knew what they had accomplished with this piece of non-political publicity — which was anything but non-political.

CHAPTER 32

INK took the lead in confronting Porter's change in rules for the White House media. Zeb Tolle was able to get an injunction by a 3 judge panel against the President and his actions — but, as he had said, the President was on the road campaigning.

The other networks, cable outlets, podcasts, and on-line producers mostly did what Porter demanded. INK was the exception.

The full press conference with the President had been shown on TV and was such a high demand piece of video on-line, INK may have had its injunction but it lost tremendously with the public.

Very humble reporters applied for new credentials after having met the President's demands. The new rules were bought into by the public, and the embarrassed media felt the sting of their error.

WHITE HOUSE MEDIA RULES

1. Journalists authorized to attend White House press events will present themselves professionally in their manner of dress, decorum, and respectful behavior;

2. Questions from the media must be based on double-sourced and complete information not merely speculation;

3. Journalists, found to be pursuing lines of questions and stories already known to be false, will be in Jeopardy of forfeiting their White House credentials;

4. A journalist called upon to ask a question will ask a single question and then will yield the floor to other journalists;

5. At the discretion of the President or other White House officials taking questions, a follow-up question or questions may be permitted; and where a follow-up has been allowed and asked, the questioner will then yield the floor;

6. "Yielding the floor" includes, when applicable, physically surrendering the microphone to White House staff as well as retaking their seat;

7. Failure to abide by any of these rules may result in suspension or revocation of the journalist's White House press pass.

There was a great deal of complaining from the media about the 1st, 2nd, and 3rd rules, but there was nothing they could do about it. INK did not get reaccredited, and their seat was given to an on-line journalism organization. This caused a drastic drop in INK viewership and a corresponding drop in advertisers. The result was that INK all but disappeared from the ratings and was soon only an empty shell. Zeb Tolle kept it alive pouring good money after squandered funds into it but within a year it closed shop completely.

❦

The final joint presidential candidate debate was on Foreign Affairs. To the surprise of no one, it was the least viewed of the debates. All three candidates held their own with questions from the three international media outlets represented — the BBC, the CBC, and Telemundo.

Both Sturges and Tossen appeared to be stiff and on edge, even though such matters in question were well within their wheel house. Porter was relaxed and gave simple, common sense answers to each topic and even questioned the assumptions of one question from the CBC. He made it clear that the US had long been open and overly generous in its relations with other nations. Furthermore, this behavior continued if somewhat more limited on his watch. The US had not become isolationist but had become more self-aware.

"The world," he said, "had long considered the US to be the world's policeman and financial savior in times of crisis. We have been a trusted ally with equals and always an enemy to be feared in cases of confrontation. The US wants a fair trade and equal opportunities for all — but not at the expense of American lives and treasure. We will be glad to lead but we will not be the patsy for anyone."

George Tossen tried his best to sound like a diplomat but came off sounding noncommittal to difficult questions. Vincent Sturges took the approach of being kind and welcoming to all — within limits. But he would not nail down what those limits were.

The end of the debate proved to be a ratings disaster and a disappointment to the voting public. No one seemed to learn anything new and no minds were changed by the exchange.

THE LAST WEEK BEFORE THE NOVEMBER ELECTION DAY, THE RATINGS polls were now mostly calling the contest a horse race. Some gave the Democrats the lead by a few points and others the Republicans. But all were within the margin of error.

Only a very few outlying poll organizations gave the lead to Porter and the Independent Party.

What had changed on the campaign trail was that now Porter and Deidra sang two songs at each outing with The Arkansas Travelers. First they always dedicated "The Reuben James" to those who lost their lives in the Amarillo VA terrorist attack. Next the President and First Lady were joined by Tracy Holyoak, to harmonize on "Shenandoah." The President had discovered that his vice presidential candidate had been in a rock band during her college years. The crowds loved it.

The final day before voting, Porter and company visited Michigan, Wisconsin, Ohio and Indiana. With that they returned to the White House to await the outcome of the voting.

RELUCTANT CANDIDATE

Election night found Porter, Deidra, Tracy and her husband, Bradley, Chief-of-Staff Graham Newcome, Cinnamon Higdon, and the rest of the White House staff in the Oval Office. Five TV's were set up and tuned to different networks, cable outlets, and even on-line services.

Coffee, cold drinks and both hot and cold tea flowed as the crowd watched and awaited the vote counts. Cinnamon had set up a large white board on a tripod in front of the fireplace with colored columns and markers to keep count of the Presidential race — including an Electoral College count box. She also had one for the two amendments and the Convention of States question.

Select groups of statisticians were punching in results of exit-poll samples in attempts to pre-guess the results prior to the closing of polls. The major networks, cable outlets, and even respected on-line sites held their calling of election results until after the polls in a state or time zone had closed. The point was not to influence voters in the other time zones too early into thinking that a candidate or issue was all but decided by voters on the East coast.

But as the results began to be announced, it was clear early on that the nation had a sense of what it wanted. Both amendments were given significant support, the Convention of State slightly less, but still a convincing win. Each party loyalist had done their best to put their faction into power and sway the results of the amendments. However, the public had seen and heard from the candidates and had their own ideas. The response was positively in favor of, and for the first time in history, the Independent Party.

Florida, a key battleground state on the East coast, was the first declared crucial win for Porter and Tracy. When bell-weather Ohio, which had correctly picked every presidential contest but one since World War 2, proved to be solidly in the Independent Party camp, there were shouts of joy in the Oval Office.

So it went all across the country. In the end only New York City, Chicago, and L.A. had committed themselves to the Democrats, but the nation as a whole was 73 percent behind the President, his amendments, and his call for a Convention of States.

Independent congressional candidates that supported the amendments, the convention, and the President also did very well. More than half of the states even chose Independent new governors.

The phone rang on the President's desk. It was a concession call from George Tossen and the Democrats. The Oval Office was clearing out as everyone went to change clothes to attend the planned celebrations when a call finally came from an obviously frustrated and angry Vincent Sturges. He said all the right words but he couldn't and didn't even try to hide his true feelings.

As the President hung up after that call, he found Cinnamon Higdon waiting for him. They were almost alone when she said, "Mr. President, I have decided I've had enough of DC."

"I can't say I'm surprised."

"I'll stay until you get a replacement or until your inauguration."

"Thank you. You are going to be a very hard act to follow. What are your plans?"

"My law school degree is equal to a Ph.D. At least in some circles."

"I understand. It is a doctorate of law."

"Well, based on that I've been offered a teaching position at the University of Missouri — in their school of journalism "

"One of the best in the nation. Congratulations." Porter offered his hand to Cinnamon which she ignored as she stepped in for a hug.

"Anything I can ever do for you, Mr. President," she said, "I will forever be in your debt."

When she stepped back, Porter said, "Well, you could find me a replacement. I understand Grant has a book deal and now is taking a job with an on-line site."

"That's what I heard. And don't be surprised if you also lose a speech writer."

"Therese Herzog?"

"She and Grant have become an item."

"There is so much I don't hear about in this bubble."

"Sometimes it's a good thing, Mr. President. Let's go party."

CHAPTER 33

Election night party venues were booked years in advance. All the big hotels and ballrooms were already claimed by the established parties. Depending on the site they were also loaded with red or blue balloons and confetti. These turned out to be sad places. The highlights in each were the concession speeches of the losers.

The Independents had to scramble to find space. They ended up using a couple of older hotels and a few university ballrooms. The Model Room at the US Patent Office was one such site, not used since Abraham Lincoln first employed it. In one case they had to book a DC high school gym. In all there were 6 celebrations.

The locations didn't matter. These were not black tie and tails events. Some were even less formal than others.

Whenever the President and First Lady as well as Vice President Elect Tracy Holyoak and her husband arrived, the places burst into cheers.

There was one celebration for White House and campaign staff. Porter made a point of introducing Ward and Ella, both of whom were well known to this crowd. This was where Porter gave his gracious and magnanimous winner's speech.

In his speech he pointed out that the nation had spoken profoundly with a call for a new direction with the amendments and call for a Convention of States.

"These must be times of careful thought and the very careful selection of representatives for the Convention. In a real sense," Porter said, "this is either a time of American Renaissance or the beginning of the end.

"Congress has been handed a couple of defeats, and the next few years will be the time when we *correct* the types of people who represent us — or we fail. What I hope is that we are on our guard not to become led by bureaucrats but people who understand that politics should not be a *class* nor a *profession* but a part time 'service' occupation."

When these remarks were greeted with thunderous applause, Porter had to wait to say his next piece.

"As revolutionary pamphleteer Thomas Paine wrote, *'These are the times that try men's souls.'* Let's make them the time which sees a rebirth in all the qualities we hold dearest as Americans. We must keep in mind that freedom is never free — justice is only justice if we demand that it is for one and all. And that shining city on the hill which is America is always in danger of being snuffed out from within as well as from without. If we can do just one thing, let it be that we recommit ourselves to a unique nation, a culture of openness and fairness to those who will willing participate, and to stand strong for ourselves and the world as the true light of liberty."

With that the President and First Lady began to dance joined by Vice President Elect and her husband and then by all in attendance.

THE PRESIDENT SPOKE PRETTY MUCH THE SAME WORDS AT EACH celebration. The liquor flowed and the food was abundant at each location. Different live bands performed at each event and there was nothing in the air but joy.

One event the featured band was The Arkansas Travelers. The high point was the singing of all the now popular songs featuring the President and First Lady and the President playing the banjo.

At the third event, primarily a joint military ball, the President was surprised to discover the now Major Ivan J. Noon had taken leave from Syria to be at this party for President Randall.

Porter proudly introduced the major to the crowd who all took it as a sign that this President was behind them 100 percent.

Formal or informal, all the events were just as joyous and celebratory as all the rest.

The President and his party traveled from function to function in caravans chosen at random. Crowds along the streets of DC who recognized the stream of black limos for what it was screamed and yelled their support — some toasting the group of cars with whatever happened to be in their hands.

The last party was the one at the high school gym. Once more Porter was surprised to find it was made up of mostly journalists. These were the famous and the unknown faces behind cameras who were heartened by the Howard Sterling's book. They were the journalists who were proud to support a President who called balls and strikes as he saw them. They even supported his new White House media rules.

Among those at the event was Cinnamon Higdon who walked up to the President arm-in-arm with Chief-of-Staff Graham Newcome.

"Is this something we should know about?" Porter asked as Deidra hugged Cinnamon.

"It's going to be long distance for a while," Graham said looking down and smiling at Cinnamon.

"I'm buying round trip tickets in bulk," she laughed.

Cinnamon then introduced the President to Howard Sterling and Saundra Fontan.

"I've been an admirer of your work for years," Porter said as they shook hands and he introduced Deidra.

"Then you should know, Mr. President, that my work is her work," Howard said gesturing to Saundra. "I am but the face and the voice. She is the brains of the operation."

"He is a liar, Mr. President," Saundra said. "I wouldn't work for him if he weren't smarter than me."

"And, I wouldn't work with her if she weren't smarter than me."

"I like the way you two think," Porter laughed.

When Howard had introduced his wife, Jennifer, Deidra said, "I liked your book."

"I'm surprised anyone still remembers it."

"I recommend it to young women all the time."

"I guess that's why I keep getting some royalty checks," Jennifer laughed.

Cinnamon stood to one side smiling. She was sure both the President and First Lady would appreciate Howard, Jennifer, and Saundra.

The meeting was, however, no accident. This was Cinnamon's surprise for Porter. Having known both Howard and Saundra over the last few years, she felt free to call them when she made up her mind to leave the White House.

"I understand you are — or soon will be —," Howard said "— in the market for some new faces in your Press Office. My producer/ co-author and I would like to offer our services."

The President glanced over at Cinnamon with his mouth open. She just winked.

"Done," Porter said shaking hands with Howard and Saundra again. "This night just keeps getting better and better."

"We'll make the transition seamless, Mr. President," Howard said. "And if there's anything we can do officially or unofficially, please feel free to call on us."

"Thank you very much," Porter said. "You realize this next term is going to be harder than the other one."

"We like a challenge," Saundra said.

"If you want to start the new year off with a bang...," Howard grinned at Saundra who only smiled to herself and shook her head. "I've been thinking you might find this amusing."

"What's that?" Porter asked.

"What if we call some of our friends in the supermarket tabloid business. I think I could get one of them to go with a headline that reads; 'PRESIDENT HAS SIX BALLS?'"

. . .

THE END

FREE E-BOOKS

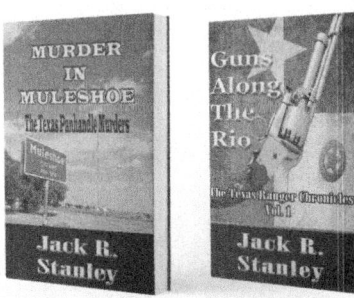

[MURDER IN MULESHOE]
There's a murderer in town. Should we track him or her down or throw a parade?
[GUNS ALONG THE RIO]
It's 1852 and two fresh off the ranch 17-year-olds join the Texas Rangers. What could possibly go wrong?

Go to: http://eepurl.com/dKEi_Y

THANKS

Thank you for taking the time to read **[THE RELUCTANT PRESI-DENT]**. *If you enjoyed it, please consider telling your friends or posting a short review.* Two to three sentences make a tremendous difference to the visibility of this book..It's important because reviews impact the algorithms at Amazon, Google and Apple. Click here to leave a short review.

Word of mouth is an author's best friend and much appreciated.
Thank you,
Jack R. Stanley

ABOUT THE AUTHOR

About The Author

Jack R. Stanley is an award winning novelist, playwright, and screenwriter. As an officer and combat photographer in Vietnam he earned the Bronze Star. Yet he says, "When you're in a firefight and everybody else on both side have guns while you have a camera --- you get to change your pants a lot."

After his military service he received both his M.A. and his Ph.D. at the University of Michigan in Ann Arbor in Radio-TV-Film. His doctoral dissertation was on the long running TV series GUNSMOKE. Stanley also received two of Michigan's most prestigious creative writing awards, The Hopwood Award, one for a one-act play and the second for a novel.

Still married to his gifted high school sweetheart, Stanley's first academic position was TV Area Head at The University of Texas at Austin's Department of Radio-TV-Film. He later moved to deep-south Texas and the Lower Rio Grande Valley for a challenging position with The University of Texas-Pan American (UTPA - now UTRGV). Here he taught Theatre-TV-Film for 30 years in the Department of Communication serving as Department Chair at U.T.P.A. for 11 years. He did take one year out to work for The University of Alaska Anchorage as a visiting professor. Back in Texas, Stanley directed for stage at The University Theatre, produced and directed fifteen student staffed, cast, and crewed feature films, writing most of the original screenplays. Just a few of his credits are available on IMDB.com.

He now lives in the Texas Panhandle where he writes his fiction.

ALSO BY JACK R. STANLEY

Novels

[Political Fiction]

The Reluctant President

The Reluctant Incumbent

[Mysteries]

Murder In Muleshoe

Corpse In Canyon

The Lovecraft Murders

[Vietnam]

Through A Lens Darkly: Vietnam

[Westerns]

Guns Along The Rio

West Of The Frio

A Hard Line Between The Rios

The Mormon Marshal

The Gavel and the Gun

Short Stories

TALES FROM THE ALASKAN GOLD RUSH

Klondike Justice

Dangerous Camp On The Kenai

The Winds of Skagway

Screenplays

6 and 10

The 7th Luger

Afternoon Delight

Angel's Revenge

Between Love And Murder

Blood Drive

Death Scene

The Defection of Grigori Dorsky

The Evil Eye

Fatty and Hearst

Gideon: The Horse That Saved Texas

Hell In Paradise

Hollowpoint

Holiday For An Assassin

Horse Thief Hollow

Incident At Lajatis

Love, Lust, & Life

Mom & Apple Pye

Pancho's Pilot

The Prometheus Peril

The Rape of Sarah Quinn

Reservations

River of Tears

Seven Reasons Why

The Thing About Love

The Texas Rattlesnake Murders

Too Good To Be True

The Vampire Rose

A Violent End

The Virgin Casanova

Plays

Antigone In Texas

Cyrano

The Last Virgin From Las Vegas

The Seven Keys

The Unwed Widow

Made in the USA
Middletown, DE
22 June 2019